THE TEMPLAR DETECTIVE

AND THE SERGEANT'S SECRET

A TEMPLAR DETECTIVE THRILLER

Also by J. Robert Kennedy

James Acton Thrillers

The Protocol
Brass Monkey
Broken Dove
The Templar's Relic
Flags of Sin
The Arab Fall
The Circle of Eight
The Venice Code
Pompeii's Ghosts
Amazon Burning
The Riddle
Blood Relics
Sins of the Titanic
Saint Peter's Soldiers
The Thirteenth Legion

Raging Sun
Wages of Sin
Wrath of the Gods
The Templar's Revenge
The Nazi's Engineer
Atlantis Lost
The Cylon Curse
The Viking Deception
Keepers of the Lost Ark
The Tomb of Genghis Khan
The Manila Deception
The Fourth Bible
Embassy of the Empire
Armageddon
No Good Deed

Special Agent Dylan Kane Thrillers

Rogue Operator
Containment Failure
Cold Warriors
Death to America
Black Widow

The Agenda
Retribution
State Sanctioned
Extraordinary Rendition
Red Eagle

The Messenger

Templar Detective Thrillers

The Templar Detective
The Parisian Adulteress
The Sergeant's Secret

The Code Breaker
The Black Scourge
The Unholy Exorcist

The Lost Children

Kriminalinspektor Wolfgang Vogel Mysteries

The Colonel's Wife   *Sins of the Child*

Delta Force Unleashed Thrillers

Payback   *Kill Chain*
Infidels   *Forgotten*
The Lazarus Moment   *The Cuban Incident*

Detective Shakespeare Mysteries

Depraved Difference   *Tick Tock*   *The Redeemer*

Zander Varga, Vampire Detective

The Turned

THE
TEMPLAR
DETECTIVE
AND THE
SERGEANT'S
SECRET

J. ROBERT KENNEDY

UnderMill PRESS

Copyright ©2018 J. Robert Kennedy

ISBN: 9781990418020

First Edition

For Lieutenant Colonel Arnaud Beltrame, who paid the ultimate price by exchanging himself for civilian hostages in Trèbes, France, proving selfless sacrifice still exists today.

THE TEMPLAR DETECTIVE

AND THE SERGEANT'S SECRET

A TEMPLAR DETECTIVE
THRILLER

THE
TEMPLAR
DETECTIVE
AND THE
SERGEANTS
SECRET

A TEMPLAR DETECTIVE

THRILLER

"Master, go on; and I will follow thee to the last gasp, with truth and loyalty."

As You Like It, Act II, Scene 3
William Shakespeare

"Nothing is more noble, nothing more venerable, than loyalty."

Cicero

AUTHOR'S NOTE

This is the third novel in this series, and for those who have read the others and embraced these characters as so many of you have, please feel free to skip this note, as you will have already read it.

The word "detective" is believed to have originated in the mid-nineteenth century, however, that doesn't mean the concept of someone who investigated crime originated less than two hundred years ago. Crime long pre-dated this era, and those who investigated it as well.

The following historical thriller is intended to be an entertaining read for all, with the concept of a "Templar Detective" a fun play on a modern term. The dialog is intentionally written in such a way that today's audiences can relate, as opposed to how people might have spoken in Medieval France, where, of course, they conversed in French and not English, with therefore completely different manners of speaking, and of addressing one another. For consistency, English phrasing is always used, such as Mister instead of Monsieur, for example. This does not mean they will be speaking to each other as rappers and gangsters, but will instead communicate in ways that imply comfort and familiarity, as we would today. If you are expecting, "Thou dost hath offended me, my good sir," then prepareth thyself for disappointment. If, however, you are looking for a fast-paced adventure, with plenty of action, mystery,

and humor, then you've come to the right place.
Enjoy.

PREFACE

In medieval France, the King used agents known as *bailli*, or bailiffs, to administer much of his realm, and as a result, these men wielded much power over the subjects they were responsible for, including collecting taxes, calling men to service, and administering the laws of the land.

These men were appointed by the King, were paid by the crown, and their entire livelihoods were dependent upon their continued employment.

Even more dependent were those they hired to assist them, known as Bailiff's Delegates, who wielded similar powers, though on a much smaller geographic scale.

And should this power be wielded in such a way that the population they were responsible for were to take offense, the livelihood of the Bailiff's Delegate could be threatened.

Unless, of course, fear ruled the hearts of those who would have cause to complain.

Kingdom of France
AD 1297

Simon Chastain roared in agony as his entire body jerked off the table, his arms and legs stretched to their limits by ropes attached to ratchets that left his naked body racked with pain as his torturer cranked the wheel yet another turn.

It was unlike anything he could have imagined, even at the hands of the Saracens.

But these weren't Saracens.

These were fellow Frenchmen.

And they weren't his brothers.

He was a Templar sergeant, and had fought in the Holy Land for the better part of two decades, but recent events had changed all that. With the death of his master's sister, he and two trusted squires had followed Sir Marcus de Rancourt back to his childhood home, and a decision had been made.

To stay and raise the orphaned children.

It had been a decision he initially supported, then doubt had set in.

Doubt that had led him here, in some unknown prison, tortured daily, for weeks on end. The pain he could endure, as it would end eventually, though for now, they were keeping him alive for some reason.

It was the solitude between these torturous sessions that would be the death of him.

His faith had prepared him for what was eventually to come, and he didn't fear it. In fact, he would welcome it after these past weeks, and if it weren't for his master and friend, he would have given up long ago.

But he couldn't let go.

Not yet.

For he had to somehow survive, so his master, his friend, Sir Marcus, would know he hadn't betrayed him. He had to make certain his master knew he had done everything he could to return to his side, his decision made.

He somehow had to get home, home to a farm only weeks ago he had cursed.

A farm that held everything he loved in the world, and worse, everything that loved him.

De Rancourt Residence
Crécy-la-Chapelle, Kingdom of France
One month earlier

"It's makeshift, but it will have to do."

Sir Marcus de Rancourt let his eyes wander around the nearly finished barracks on the farm he now called home. With the death of his sister, several months ago he and his trusted men, Sergeant Simon Chastain, and squires David and Jeremy, had all agreed to remain, giving up the life of brotherhood in the Poor Fellow-Soldiers of Christ and of the Temple of Solomon—the Knights Templar.

Though they hadn't truly given it up. They had been granted special dispensation to remain members of the Order, and remain on the farm. It was a difficult life, but life as a Templar was also difficult, though in different ways, in ways they all knew and loved.

Farm life was different, and he wasn't yet convinced he could ever love it.

Tanya, the farm's mastiff, charged into the barracks, barking happily, as the children he was now responsible for, chased her, giggling and laughing, as happy as he had ever seen them. Jacques and Angeline, his late sister's children, were in the lead, their cheeks red, their hair filled with snowflakes, and Pierre, an orphan they had taken in after his parents' murder, followed, gasping for breath, though clearly content.

They disappeared in short order.

6

"We need a door."

The others chuckled at Simon's observation as they all sat around the stone fireplace that, try as it might, could only take some of the chill out of the winter air, the structure still far too drafty.

Marcus regarded his friend. "Tomorrow we'll put one on. The extension to the house is finished, and Lady Joanne is now settled with her chambermaid. We can now return our attention to our own accommodations."

David, the eldest of the two squires, eyed him. "Did you say 'our?'"

Marcus smiled. "Yes, I did. Now that we have two women living with us, the children don't need me in the house, and I fear what the townsfolk might think should I be staying under the same roof as them."

Simon grunted. "They wouldn't dare say anything, if I have anything to say about it."

Marcus laughed, slapping his friend on the back. "My honor is always secure with you around." He stared through the open door and down at the house left him by his sister and brother-in-law, Henri. Henri was the connection he had with Lady Joanne de Rohan, a woman who had lost everything after accusations of adultery just weeks ago. Forced from her home, he had offered her a place to stay, an offer she had happily accepted.

He had to admit it was a relief.

Though he was anything but comfortable around women, he was even less so around children.

He knew nothing about either.

But Lady Joanne had taken to the children immediately, as had her trusted chambermaid,

7

Beatrice, and their presence had mercifully reduced the attentions of the young Isabelle Leblanc, a friend of his late sister's who had taken care of the children along with her mother, while they awaited his return from the Holy Land.

And Isabelle was a constant source of delight for his men, who teased him mercilessly about her apparent desire to take him for a husband.

She was a beautiful woman, even he wasn't blind to that, but he was a warrior monk, sworn to poverty and celibacy, and as he remained a Templar, he was still bound by those vows.

Lady Joanne's voice called out, announcing dinner, and the children bolted toward the house.

Somebody screamed.

They all leaped to their feet, rushing out the door, to see Pierre tumbling down the slope, then rolling to his knees, laughing as he brushed the snow off himself, Jacques standing with his fists on his hips, apparently having pushed him.

"What did I tell you about that?" cried Joanne, wagging a finger. "Someone is going to get hurt one of these days if you're not careful!"

"Or killed."

Marcus glanced at Simon and frowned, his friend's face clouded over, his eyes glistening, his gaze unfocused, as if he were staring back at some distant memory. "Are you all right?"

Simon sighed then nodded. "Just remembering something."

"What?"

Simon shook his head. "Nothing I care to talk about." He stabbed a finger toward the children.

8

"They just don't listen. How many times has she told Jacques to stop shoving Pierre?"

David stared after the children as they raced inside the house. "I think he's jealous. He's just trying to establish his dominance over Pierre, so that he knows his place." David shoved Jeremy, tripping him with a strategically placed foot. "Like Jeremy knows I'm his better."

Jeremy stared up at him. "I hear there's a witch in the woods. Maybe I'll seek her out in the morning and make sure she puts a curse on you."

David glanced around, his hands palms up, and shrugged. "What more can she do to me?"

Marcus frowned, David noticing, his jaw dropping with the realization of what he had said.

"I'm sorry, sir, I didn't mean it like that, I was just joking around."

Marcus nodded, but knew his squire was telling him only half the truth. None of them were truly happy. This was not the life they were used to. They were all Templars of varying ranks, all devoted to the brotherhood, and now, thanks to his decision, and their undying loyalty to him, he had condemned them all to a life toiling on a farm, raising children, and protecting the growing brood that now called the humble property home.

David's head dropped. "I'll go get us our dinner." Jeremy scrambled after him, clearly not wanting to stick around for whatever might be said next. Marcus turned back toward the barracks and glanced over his shoulder at Simon, following a few paces behind.

"And what do *you* think?"

Simon's eyebrows rose slightly. "Of what?"

9

"Of this new life."

"I've told you that my place is at your side."

"And if it weren't?"

Simon looked away, as if ashamed of what he might say.

"Out with it, my friend. If I can't trust you to tell me the truth, then whom can I?"

Simon sighed as they stepped through the open doorway. "I can't say that I'd choose this life."

"What would you choose?"

Simon sat on the edge of his bed, the private rooms Marcus had promised them all, yet to be completed, and until each had their own room, they had all agreed to continue to share. "I can feel it in my bones that I'm no longer the warrior I once was. The journey back to the Holy Land would be long and arduous, and I'd be just that much older by the time I got back there."

"So you would stay in France?"

Simon nodded. "Now that I'm here, yes. If we had never left, I'd have been content to die on the sands our Lord once roamed."

Marcus shivered against the cold. "I never thought I'd miss the heat, but days like today make me yearn for the desert sun."

Simon grunted. "This will be my first winter in France since I was a boy."

"You grew up not far from here, didn't you?"

Simon stared out the door. "A few days' ride. On the other side of Paris."

"Is your family still there?"

Simon shrugged. "No idea."

10

Marcus stared at his friend. In all the years he had known Simon, the man had barely mentioned his home. All Marcus knew was that he apparently had a brother, and that he hadn't seen nor spoken to any of his family since he left as a boy. In fact, Marcus didn't even know why he had left.

"Can I ask you something?"

Simon regarded him, his eyes suggesting he wanted to say no, as if he knew what Marcus was about to ask him. "Of course."

"Why did you leave?"

Simon looked away, but not before a hint of shame revealed itself. "It's not something I want to talk about."

"I'll respect your privacy, my friend. But whatever the reason, it clearly bothers you." Marcus steeled himself for what was to come next, for he feared what the response might be. "And clearly life here has you troubled." He leaned forward, placing a hand on his friend's shoulder. "You have been my brother for longer than I can remember. There is no one that I trust more than you, or love more than you. And it pains me to see you unhappy."

Simon turned back toward him, staring him in the eyes. "You shame me with your words."

Marcus' chest ached at the pain in his friend's voice. He leaned back, removing his hand. "Our work here is done for the season. All that is left is to finish the barracks, and tend the animals. It is work that can be done without you. I propose you go visit your family, and settle whatever business you have with them from so long ago."

Simon's mouth opened to respond, a response that

Marcus was certain would be a rejection of his suggestion.

He held up a finger, cutting Simon off. "Go to your family, settle your business with them, and then make your decision as to what you want to do with your life. Whether that is to return to the Holy Land to serve the Order, leave the farm to serve the Order in some other way, remain with your family, or to return here, I will support your decision, no matter what." He leaned forward once again, lowering his voice. "My friend, I release you from any obligations you might have toward me. Go, seek out your family. Settle any past grievances, then with a clear conscience, decide for once in your life what is best for Simon, rather than what is best for those around you."

Simon's shoulders slumped, and as his friend drew in several deep, slow breaths, it was clear he was struggling to maintain control. Marcus desperately wanted to ask him once again what was bothering him, but held off, knowing his friend needed his space right now to maintain his dignity.

Something had happened when Simon was a child. What it was, he wasn't sure, but it had happened when he was young, perhaps not even ten years of age. All Marcus knew was that Simon had left home and met up with a group of Templars heading for the Holy Land. They had taken him in, assuming he was orphaned, and he had trained to become a squire, then eventually a sergeant.

Precious little information to go on.

But recently, there were hints of something more. The horseplay between his nephew Jacques, and the orphan Pierre, seemed to trouble Simon, especially when Jacques, larger than the slight Pierre, dominated him. Simon never said anything, but Marcus knew his friend well enough to know when he was restraining himself. Fortunately, Lady Joanne's introduction into their growing family provided a firm voice to admonish the young Jacques, and Simon's unconscious head bobbing betrayed his feelings on the matter.

Did something happen when you were young? Something surrounding children bullying each other?

David and Jeremy entered the room carrying a large pot of stew and two loaves of bread. They hooked the pot over the fire then grabbed Marcus' and Simon's bowls sitting on a shelf near the hearth. David handed his master a full, steaming bowl of what smelled like something delicious. Marcus took it, then the chunk of bread held out for him.

"Thanks."

David curtsied in a manner any lady would be proud of, as Jeremy held out Simon's meal, the old warrior ignoring him. "Sergeant?"

Nothing.

Jeremy kicked Simon in the shin, finally getting his attention. "Where were you?"

Simon grunted, taking the food, before looking at Marcus sheepishly. "The other side of Paris, I believe."

Marcus nodded in understanding. His friend had made his decision. He would be leaving them.

Now the question was whether he would ever return.

13

Approaching Le Chesnay, Kingdom of France
Three days after leaving the farm

Simon Chastain stared at the barren, snow-covered landscape surrounding him. France could be a desolate place when it wanted to be, though nothing compared to the Holy Land. The trees along the way, their leaves long having given up their hold, could be mistaken for the drought-ridden branches with which he was so familiar.

Except for the white.

It was everywhere, the only break the pine trees of the forest, and the mud of the well-traveled road upon which he now found himself.

And none of it looked even remotely familiar.

As a boy, he had never left his village. Not once. He remembered his family was poor. Very poor. But never hungry. His father worked the farm hard, sacrificing a portion of his crops to pay the rent, the rest used to feed the family or trade for what was needed. And in the winter, when the farm was frozen over, he remembered his father working odd jobs, a very handy carpenter.

And his mother.

His chest ached at the thought of her. All he could remember of her was her smile, and the wonderful smells that would come from the kitchen. Her baked goods were in high demand, he recalled, not only among his friends, but the townsfolk as well, her wares helping supply several taverns in the area, weary travelers blessed with her homemade goods.

14

Though perhaps the life he remembered wasn't as idyllic as he now imagined. As with most memories, only the best and worst were usually retained over time. The mundane was forgotten, the day-to-day misery shoved to the far recesses of the mind.

Only the triumphs and tragedies were retained from those times. He remembered skinning his knees, spraining an ankle, cracking his head on a rock.

And the death of one young boy.

And what Simon's father had thought of his own son.

Le Chesnay, Kingdom of France
AD 1266
31 Years Earlier

"Hey! What did I tell you? *Don't* touch the shirt!"

Simon shook his head at Gilles Laurent. The shirt was impressive. Unlike any he had ever before seen. And it definitely shouldn't be worn when horsing around. It was apparently from Paris, a city he had only heard of, and desperately wanted to see. He hoped to one day. He dreamed of exploring its streets as a young man, when he had escaped the clutches of his parents, and experiencing the life he had heard described by those traveling through their small town.

But there was time for that.

Plenty of time.

After all, he had just turned ten, and according to his older brother, until he had hair on his penis, he wasn't a real man. He wasn't so sure about that. He knew he wasn't a man. That wasn't the problem. But hair on his penis? The very idea sounded like nonsense. He didn't have a hair anywhere except on his head. Why would God choose to put it on one's penis as well?

His brother was always playing pranks on him, so he believed only about half of what he told him.

Or rather, he should.

He was always falling for his brother's lies.

He sighed. "Can I ask you guys something?"

Gilles stopped, as did Christian Samuel, whose

finger was in midair, ready to touch the forbidden shirt ever so gently, and Roland Villeneuve, who was snickering uncontrollably.

Gilles looked at him. "What?"

"Well, my brother says that when we get older, we're going to get hair on our penises."

Christian and Roland's eyes bulged in shock, but Gilles nodded. "It's true."

Simon's eyes shot wide as well. "It is?"

"Yes, but not on it, around it. In fact, I've got hair already."

Everyone gathered around Gilles. "Show us!"

"I'm not showing you!"

"Come on!" pleaded Simon. "I want to see!"

"Yes! Show us!" urged the others.

Gilles, a couple of years older than the rest, shrugged. "Fine. But if you tell anyone, I'll kill you."

And he dropped his pants.

All three boys leaned closer, their heads mere inches from Gilles' private parts. Simon twisted his head and looked up at Gilles. "Where's the hair?"

Gilles glared at him. "What are you talking about? It's right here." He reached down and pulled at something to the side of his member.

Simon laughed. "*One* hair!"

Gilles yanked his pants up, blushing. "Yes, well it's one more than you've apparently got!"

Christian pointed. "Gilles' got one hair! Gilles' got one hair!"

Gilles took a swing at Christian, but the younger boy managed to dodge it, continuing his taunts, Gilles' face getting redder by the moment.

17

It was turning into rage.

And that was never something you wanted. Not with Gilles.

Simon motioned for Roland to back off, and was about to call an end to the taunts, when Gilles lashed out, shoving Christian hard with two hands to the chest. Christian reached out as he fell backward, his right hand gripping the shirtsleeve of Gilles' fine imported silk shirt.

The tearing of the fabric was shocking, and jaws dropped all around.

As Christian continued to fall backward.

He slammed onto the ground, the impact sounding oddly hollow.

Then he disappeared with a scream.

They all rushed to the side of the hole now revealed, Simon reaching it first and peering over the edge.

"Christian! Are you all right?"

But there was no response.

Simon looked at the others. "Can you see him?"

Gilles and Roland both shook their heads. Simon leaned in farther, squinting into the darkness that stretched out below them, the rock-lined walls revealing what this hole once was.

A well.

An abandoned well, apparently, and judging by how the wood covering it had snapped so easily, abandoned long ago.

"Christian!"

The only response was the echo of his own voice.

Roland pointed. "Wait! I see him!"

Simon peered into the darkness and noticed his eyes were slowly adjusting. Then he gasped. Christian was lying in a heap at the bottom of the well, his neck twisted, his tongue hanging out, his eyes wide and still.

He was dead.

He had to be.

Simon had seen enough death on the farm to recognize the look.

And it terrified him.

He pushed to his feet. "We have to go get help!" He turned to leave when Gilles grabbed him by the arm.

"No!"

Simon jerked his arm free. "What do you mean, no?"

Gilles shook his head. "You fool! He's dead! If we tell anyone, we'll get in trouble."

Simon stared at him, mouth agape, then snapped his jaw shut. "You mean *you'll* get in trouble. We didn't push him, *you* did!"

Gilles stepped closer. "What are you saying?"

Simon recognized the tone in the older boy. It was one he had heard before from him, and it usually ended in a good beating, a beating that would always go unpunished, as Gilles' father was the Bailiff's Delegate for the area. He was the law.

And Mr. Laurent never punished his own son, and never doubted his own son's word.

But surely, this time, he would have to punish him.

After all, Christian was dead, by Gilles' hand.

Gilles gave Simon a shove. "I asked you a question! What are you saying?"

Simon stepped backward. "Me and Roland did nothing wrong. You're the one who pushed him, not us."

Gilles' cheeks and ears went red and his nostrils flared. He advanced, and Simon prepared for the beating of a lifetime.

Then Gilles stopped, a smile creeping up from the corners of his mouth.

"You did it."

Simon's eyes widened, confused. "What?"

"That's what I'm going to tell them. You did it."

Simon's eyes widened further, exchanging a horrified glance with Roland. "But I didn't touch him!"

"I don't care." Gilles' smug expression was terrifying, for Simon knew why it was there. Gilles was always believed by his father, and his father was the only law the town had.

No one would believe the poor son of a poorer farmer.

"They-they'll never believe you."

Gilles laughed, tossing his head back. "Who do you think they're going to believe? Me, the son of the Bailiff's Delegate? Or you, the pathetic son of an even more pathetic farmer who can barely feed and clothe his own family."

A rage formed in the pit of Simon's stomach at the insults levied against his father. He pushed it down, as this wasn't the time to defend his family's honor. There were more pressing matters at hand. He pointed at Roland. "Roland knows what happened. It'll be two against one."

Gilles sneered, walking toward a now cowering Roland. "Roland knows that I'll kill him if he doesn't say exactly what I want him to say." He grabbed Roland by the back of the neck, dragging him toward the open well. "Do you want to join him?"

"N-no!"

"Then who pushed Christian?"

"S-Simon did."

Gilles let go of Roland's neck, a smile of pure evil spreading. "There, you see? Two against one."

Simon stepped slowly backward, his head shaking uncontrollably. "You'll never get away with this! It's not fair!"

Gilles grunted. "Like my father always says, 'who said life was supposed to be fair?'" One side of his nose curled up. "They're going to hang you when they find out." Gilles started to laugh, pointing his finger at Simon. "You're going to be swinging from a tree before the sun sets!"

Simon stared at Gilles in horror, then at Roland, nervously joining in on Gilles' laughter.

Settling the matter.

Simon turned and sprinted away from the well, heading for the trees, checking over his shoulder repeatedly for any signs of pursuit, but there was none. He hid in the tree line, turning back to watch Gilles and Roland cover up the abandoned well with the broken wood, then several tree branches.

Then as the two boys ran toward the town, Simon realized he had made a grave mistake.

He should have run toward home, rather than away from it, for getting the truth out first would be his only hope.

21

They are *going to hang me.*

His stomach flipped and he bent over as he emptied his stomach contents onto the forest floor. He spat, wiping his mouth on the back of his sleeve, then raced after the others.

It didn't take long to reach the small town they all called home. He had always been happy here, despite his dreams of Paris, and Sundays, like today, were when he was happiest. After church, the entire town would gather, then later, he'd return to the family home, and with no one working, they would all sit around the fire and listen to stories expertly told by his father, until they were all falling asleep in each other's arms.

It was a great life, a life that today was working against him.

For everyone but the children were still in the church, and that was where Gilles and Roland were heading.

There would be no way to head them off, or get to his own parents first, to tell them his side of the story.

Gilles burst through the doors, and Simon could hear, even from this distance, the words that would change his life forever.

"Simon killed Christian!"

"What?" cried someone, a woman, but Simon couldn't be sure who.

He reached the church, but instead of going inside, ran around to the back, out of sight of the road and any who might come outside searching for him. He pressed his eye against a gap between the boards, staring at those inside as they gathered around the new arrivals.

22

Gilles' parents pushed through the crowd, his father an imposing figure that helped in his job as Bailiff's Delegate. "What's going on here?"

Christian's parents followed in Mr. Laurent's wake.

"What's happened to Christian?" asked the boy's mother.

"There was a fight!" explained Gilles, quickly spilling out the lie he had obviously rehearsed on his way here. "Simon pushed him and he fell into—"

Gilles' mother cried out. "What happened to your shirt?"

Mr. Laurent stared at his wife. "I hardly think his shirt matters at a time like this!"

The look she gave him made it clear she disagreed, but Simon wasn't paying that any mind. There was a hole in Gilles' story, a hole Simon couldn't possibly see how the liar could explain.

And Gilles knew it, his eyes bulging as he was probably remembering for the first time that Christian had torn the shirt when he fell.

Then Simon's heart sank as Gilles proved quick on his feet.

"Simon tore it when I tried to stop him from getting away!"

Mr. Laurent beamed as he wrapped an arm around his son's shoulders. "Such a brave boy! You'll make a fine Bailiff's Delegate someday."

Gilles smiled up at his father. "Thanks, Father!"

Christian's father broke up the moment. "My son! Where is he?"

And again, Simon smiled. Christian lay at the bottom of a well, with the shirtsleeve still in his hand.

Surely if they recovered the body, it would prove Gilles was lying.

And again, his hopes were dashed.

"I-I'm sorry, Mr. Samuel. Simon pushed him into the river. He went through the ice and was swept away."

Mrs. Samuel gasped out a cry. "He might be still alive! We have to find him!"

Mr. Samuel hugged his wife. "She's right. We don't know if he's dead. We must send search parties at once and search both sides of the river."

Mr. Laurent shook his head. "It's late, and we'll never find him in the dark."

Mrs. Samuel sobbed. "But we have to try!"

Mr. Laurent placed a hand on the woman's shoulder. "And we will, you have my word, but not until the morning. We can't risk anyone else falling in the river."

"Wh-what about Simon?"

Simon's chest ached at his mother's voice. It sounded meek. Ashamed.

Mr. Laurent frowned. "He must be found and made to pay for his crimes."

Mr. Samuel glared at Simon's parents. "If my boy dies, then so does yours. I want him hanged until he's dead!"

Simon's mother cried out then fainted, his father catching her before she hit the floor, as those surrounding them agreed with the sentence just pronounced.

But that wasn't what broke Simon's heart.

It was his father's face.

It was the shame on it.

But that wasn't all.

For there was more.

He was nodding with the others, agreeing with their demands that his own son pay for a crime he never committed.

Simon backed slowly away from the church, then scrambled toward the forest behind the village, and as soon as he was certain he couldn't be seen, broke out into a sprint.

Leaving behind the only life he had ever known.

Le Chesnay, Kingdom of France
AD 1297
Three days after leaving the farm

Simon shivered. He wasn't sure if it was from the bitter cold, or the bitter memories. Or perhaps a little of both. For while the landscape had meant little to him on his way back home, the town itself did. It was bigger now, though how much of that was from his limited viewpoint as a child, or actual growth, he couldn't be sure. The church hadn't changed, though the cross at the top of the steeple appeared new. There was a second blacksmith, and at least two stables and several inns that he could see, along with artisans and craftsmen hawking their wares along the only road in and out of the town.

Business was good.

And that might explain the traffic he was witnessing, something he didn't remember from his youth. Carts laden with goods, travelers on horseback passing through the town, many stopped at stalls peddling wares that those heading elsewhere might need.

It would appear that Le Chesnay had turned into a supply depot of sorts. He kept an eye out for the Templar flag, hoping he might get lucky, but spotted none. Tomorrow he'd seek out the nearest outpost so he could have a message sent back to Sir Marcus informing him that he had successfully arrived.

It was the next message he was dreading, for he had no clue what it might contain.

He wasn't happy on the farm, though he wasn't sure why. Marcus was his master, but also the best friend he had ever known. He even enjoyed David and Jeremy's company. The women now living on the farm were tolerable, though a distraction to the younger of their group, but it was thanks to them that they were actually getting fed on a regular basis, and things were organized. It was clear that Lady Joanne had managed her former substantial household efficiently, and that her chambermaid, Beatrice, was equally competent.

Their talents were wasted at the farm, though their choices were limited.

It was the children that were the bother. He had never been exposed to them before. The life of a Templar meant a life surrounded by men, not boys. The youngest, perhaps not much older than Jacques, were there to train. They worked hard, and there was little time for play.

When taken in on the road probably not far from here, he had been starving, freezing, and near death. The Templars that saved him nursed him back to health over the coming days, then were about to hand him off to an orphanage when he had pleaded with them to take him with them.

He was convinced the only reason they did, was that one of the squires had recently expired, and there was a need for someone to do the work. He had been accepted, reluctantly due to his age, but had worked hard, proving himself just as competent as the others. And by the time they reached the Holy Land almost a year later, he had grown several inches, had put on a good chunk of muscle, and a proud patch of

27

manliness was forming down below.

He chuckled at Gilles' single hair, the memory almost forgotten after all these years.

A memory surrounded by so many more painful ones.

He passed the office that had once housed the Bailiff's Delegate, and tensed, a feeling that surprised him. It had been three decades. Surely, Gilles' family had moved on.

Yet why would they?

They weren't Templars, moving from post to post, wherever they were needed. This was a town, populated by people who had likely been born here, and were destined to die here, most having never traveled more than a day's ride by horse.

He would be the rare exception, one of the few who had escaped this place he used to call home, a place that had betrayed him.

He stared at the faces lining the streets, everyone now ogling him, his black sergeant's tunic with bright red cross, evidently a rare sight in these parts, and perhaps not the wisest of things to have worn should he have wanted to remain unnoticed.

But it was too late for a change of clothes.

He sought a familiar face among the stares, though why he would expect any was beyond him. Three decades. Many of the adults he had known would be long dead, and the children long grown up.

His heart skipped a beat as he spotted a shock of bright red hair behind one of the stalls.

He only knew one person with hair like that, or rather two. Roland and his father.

He leaned forward in his saddle slightly, staring at the man, his age, trying to imagine what a boy of ten would look like now. The man turned, finally noticing the stranger attracting everyone's attention, and returned the stare.

Simon couldn't resist.

He brought his horse to a halt, looking down at the man. "You wouldn't happen to be Roland Villeneuve, would you?"

The man nodded. "I would be."

Simon dismounted and removed his glove, extending a hand, and lowering his voice. "I am Simon Chastain."

Roland stared at him blankly for a moment, then his eyes flared, though only briefly. He shook the forgotten hand, then drew Simon in closer. "You shouldn't have come back."

Simon frowned, his entire body tensing as if preparing for battle. "I would speak with you, if you have time."

Roland nodded. "Do you remember where my childhood home was?"

Simon thought for a moment before replying, much having changed, though the basic layout still the same. "I do."

"I will meet you there shortly."

Simon mounted his horse and continued slowly through the town center, questioning the wisdom of returning, Roland's words echoing in his head.

Three decades.

Apparently, it hadn't been enough time.

And why should it have been? He had almost

forgotten, the memories flooding back with the horseplay of Jacques and Pierre. His dreams had become nightmares, dominated for weeks by the scream of young Christian, by the sight of his mangled body at the bottom of the well, and the heartbreaking nods of agreement delivered by his father, condemning him to death.

Marcus' idea of returning here was a mistake.

He should have buried his memories as he had done all those years ago, and toughed it out like the soldier he was. Prayer and hard work were what was needed, not self-pity and loathing, and a trip down memory lane.

This was foolish.

He was tempted to turn around, but he was nearing the edge of the town, Roland's home up on the right, and the crowds staring at him thinning.

He tied up his horse and waited, Roland arriving only moments later by foot. He opened the door and urged him inside without saying anything. He closed the door, Simon's eyes taking a moment to adjust. He bowed to a woman who stood in the far corner.

"This is my wife, Cateline. Do you remember her?"

Cateline curtsied as Simon searched his memory for the name. He smiled and bowed. "Of course! My Lord, how you've grown!"

She stared at him curiously.

"My love, this is Simon Chastain."

It was her turn to be shocked. "The one who killed—" She stopped herself. "Forgive me. I shouldn't have said anything. It isn't my place."

Simon waved off her apology. "Don't worry, you haven't offended me, and this is your home where you should feel free to express any thought you might have, without hesitation." He stared at the floor. "But I will correct you on one thing. I killed no one, and your husband, I trust, will confirm that."

Roland stepped over to his wife, putting an arm around her shoulders. "It's true. He's innocent."

"But everyone who has ever told me the story said you confirmed it was Simon that pushed Christian into the river. Are you saying that was a lie?"

Roland's head drooped in shame. "I'm sorry, my love, but I was young and scared. Gilles threatened to kill me if I said any different, and when Simon disappeared, I figured what harm was there in perpetuating the lie? He was gone, and couldn't be hurt by it."

Cateline patted him on his chest. "But his parents. They've had to live with the burden of thinking their son was a murderer, and a coward for running away rather than facing judgment."

Roland's voice cracked. "That was the worst part of it, and for the part I played, I fear I will burn for eternity."

Simon stepped closer to his old friend. "What of my parents? Do they live?"

Roland smiled and nodded. "They do, though they are both, I fear, reaching the end."

"And my brother?"

Roland's face clouded over. "I think that is a question best answered by your parents. They would want you to hear it from them."

Simon frowned, his chest tightening. "Then the news isn't good."

"I'm afraid not."

Simon sighed. He had expected his parents might be dead, but never had he thought his brother. He glanced out the window behind him, toward the town. "And whatever became of Gilles?"

Roland lowered his voice, fear conquering his face. "After his father passed, he took over as Bailiff's Delegate." He lowered his voice even further. "And things have not been the same since. This is why I said you shouldn't have returned. Gilles played himself up as the hero after you left, his story of how he fought to try and keep you from running away taking on grander proportions every time it was told. He used it to manipulate those who might think he was nothing but a bully, and when it was time, no one dared object to the boyhood hero replacing his father."

"So the town is still convinced that I killed Christian."

"They are, to a one, though I think your parents have doubts."

Simon thought back on that night, the memory of his father's reaction burned into his mind still crushing him. "I somehow doubt that." He drew a deep breath. "Though perhaps it is time for the truth to come out."

Roland gasped, holding his wife tighter. "That wouldn't be wise. Though you may remember Gilles as a young bully, the child he was is nothing compared to the man he has become. You must leave at once, before he finds out you are here, for I fear he'll kill you if he thinks you might threaten the hold he has over these people."

Simon frowned, shaking his head. "I must see my family first. No one man will run me out of my own home, when thousands of Saracens failed to do the same."

Chastain Residence
Le Chesnay, Kingdom of France

At this very moment, Simon would rather have faced a dozen rabid Saracens, than the two people he expected on the other side of the door in front of him.

He inhaled deeply then knocked.

And cringed as the third hard rap echoed across the frozen landscape, his announcement of his presence far too loud.

Shuffling inside had his heart hammering, and the door soon opened, revealing a decrepit old man, hunched over slightly, squinting up at him.

"And who might you be?"

"Would you be Mr. Chastain?"

"I would. And again I ask my question."

Simon's chest ached as his stomach flipped. No matter how old, he'd recognize his own father, but it was the sight of his mother shuffling toward him that finally broke him, and as his face sagged and his eyes filled with tears, his mother's mouth opened and her eyes shot wide as she recognized her boy like only a mother could.

"Simon!"

His father's head spun toward her, then back at him, the old man squinting even harder, his eyesight evidently fading. He reached out and grabbed Simon's arm. "Could it be? Is it?"

Simon nodded. "It is I, your son."

His father grabbed him and pulled him close,

burying his head in Simon's chest as his mother grabbed them both, wrapping her arms around them. He closed his eyes and his chest heaved in unison with his parents, parents he hadn't seen in thirty years, parents he had resigned himself to never seeing again.

Yet here he was, embracing them once more, and much to his surprise, all apparently forgiven.

His father was first to let go and step back, but that only gave his mother more room to grab him as if she would never let him go again.

"In or out, woman, but the door closes."

His mother let go, beaming up at him and stepped back. Simon entered then closed the door behind him, the firelight revealing to his parents, perhaps for the first time, just how large he had grown, and his Templar regalia.

"A Templar!" gasped his father. "I would never have guessed." He reached out and ran a hand across the black surcoat. "And a sergeant no less." His smile broadened. "Much better than those nobles and their knighthoods, in my opinion."

Simon chuckled. "Unless things have changed around here, I doubt I'll ever have to worry about being called 'sir.'"

His father smiled and gestured at his gear. "Make yourself comfortable, son. You're home now."

Simon's chest ached again with the words.

Home.

It had been three decades, yet as he removed his heavy equipment, examining his boyhood home, precious little had changed.

He *was* home.

It just felt right, and it threatened to overwhelm him with guilt, for his home should be at his master's side, at the farm with the others, where he had sworn his devotion.

Yet that was why he was here, wasn't it? To choose his own path, with Marcus' blessing, even if that path were divergent from his friend's, from the oath he had sworn?

He sat on a chair opposite his parents, his mother fidgeting with excitement, his father squinting through the dim light. They sat in silence for a moment, no one daring speak lest they awake from the dream.

Simon broke the silence. "I met Roland on the way here. He mentioned there was grim news of Marc."

Their faces clouded over, his mother's head lowering as she stifled a sob, leaving his father to respond.

"Your brother died shortly after you left."

Simon tensed. "How?"

"He insisted on going after you, convinced he could find you. He thought you had gone to Paris, since you were always talking about wanting to see it. On the way, he encountered a group of men accosting a woman, having their way with her, they were. He tried to stop them, but he was just a boy, and they killed him for his efforts, though the girl was able to escape. It was through her that we found out what happened."

Simon sighed, his eyes closing as his shoulders sagged. "He's dead because of me." He stared from one to the other. "I'm so sorry. You lost two sons, and it's all my fault." He paused, then asked hopefully, "Do I have any other brothers or sisters?"

His father crushed his hopes with the shake of his head. "No, losing two children was enough. Your mother couldn't bear to lose another."

Simon sighed, his voice cracking. "I-I'm truly sorry."

"You should never have run away. You should have faced your accusers, and let justice prevail."

Simon nodded slowly. "Yes, I should have, but there was no justice to be had that night. I would have been hanged the moment they laid eyes on me." He dropped his eyes to the floor, lowering his voice. "And with your blessing."

His father gasped, his mother crying out in horror.

"How could you say such a thing?" she sobbed. "Your own father!"

"I was there, on the other side of the wall of the church. I saw you both, and I saw father nodding in agreement with those who said I must die."

His father stared at him, eyes wide, mouth agape. "I did no such thing!"

"I saw you."

"Then it was involuntary. The actions of a man who knew not what was going on. Do you have any children?"

Simon tapped his Templar cross. "Of course not."

"Then you can never understand the shock and horror of hearing your son has committed a murder. From the moment the accusation was made, I was in a fog. I barely remember the rest of that day."

"So you didn't believe them?"

"Of course not! You're my son! And that Gilles is a lying bastard. I wouldn't trust anything that came out of his mouth. Never have, never will."

A wave of relief swept over Simon, goosebumps raising the hairs on his arms, as one of the biggest regrets of his life, the pain he had caused his parents, was at least partially lifted. He wiped the tears away that threatened to escape, then smiled at them. "I'm sorry I ran away."

His father sighed, shaking his head. "You probably did the right thing. You're right. There was no justice to be had that night, and by the time things settled down, you would have already been swinging from a tree. The town wanted blood that night, and only yours would do." His father smiled at him, gesturing toward the cross emblazoned on Simon's chest. "You have no idea how proud I am of you, son." He beamed at his wife. "Our son, a Templar!"

She reached out and squeezed her husband's hand, not for a moment breaking her stare. "If only we had known you were well all these years."

The euphoria of the moment was swept away, remorse resettling. "I was a foolish boy, and I regret the pain I caused you, and I most earnestly regret the death of my brother because of me." He sighed, staring at the shuttered window, back toward the farm where his comrades awaited his decision, and to the deserts of the Holy Land, where he had always assumed he would die. "So many regrets."

"Well, you're home now, and tomorrow we will clear all this nonsense up."

Simon returned his attention to his father. "Roland says everyone still thinks I did it."

"Of course they do, because nobody has ever told them different. That little devil Roland! All he had to do was tell the truth that night, and everything would be different now. You'd have never run away, your brother would be alive, and that insufferable Gilles wouldn't be Bailiff's Delegate, terrorizing the town."

"Poor Mrs. Samuel. I think she's still convinced her son is alive out there, somewhere, swept away by the river, too far to ever return."

Simon regarded her. "You mean they never found the body?"

She shook her head. "They searched for weeks, up and down the river. Messages were sent to every town downriver, but nothing was ever heard. Everyone knew he was dead, but she refused to believe it." She wiped her nose with a handkerchief. "That poor woman. I know exactly how she felt. I always figured you had found some way to survive, that you were out there alive somewhere, and I always held out hope that one day you would return to us."

Simon flashed a smile, but his face was soon grim once again. "Christian never fell in the river."

Both sets of eyes widened, and his parents leaned forward in their chairs. "What?" they both cried.

"Gilles pushed Christian into an abandoned well on the old Tremblay property, just outside of town. He fell through the boards that were covering it, and broke his neck."

His father turned a bright red with rage. "But that's impossible! Even Roland said he was pushed into the river. Why lie about that?" He threw up his arms. "This is unbelievable!"

"Gilles threatened to kill him if he told the truth, so Roland had no choice but to go along with him. Everyone was terrified of Gilles as children."

His father growled. "Some things haven't changed in that respect." He clenched his fists, slamming them onto the arms of his chair. "We need to let somebody know what really happened that day, but whom?"

Simon frowned. "Normally one would tell the Bailiff's Delegate, but since that's Gilles, we'd have to go to someone outside of the town. And once you start dealing with those types of people, they couldn't care less about what happened thirty years ago in some small town they've probably barely heard of."

His father pulled at his mustache. "We must think. I will *not* have the people of this town thinking my son is a murderer, when he is nothing of the sort." He eyed the Templar tunic, then his son. "If you are willing to risk it, then I suggest we go to the town square tomorrow, and declare the truth to all who will listen."

"And Gilles?"

"Damn him to Hell. In the morning, we'll collect Roland, and tell everyone that my son, a Templar and a man of God, has returned, and that Gilles is the murderer who should have been condemned, not my son."

His mother looked petrified with the idea. "But how will we prove it?"

His father smiled. "Easy. Show them where the body is."

Roland Villeneuve Residence
Le Chesnay, Kingdom of France

Roland stared about the empty house. It was a humble home, generations old, with a separate bedroom added about a decade ago that had made all the difference with three kids. But it was here, in the common area, where they all gathered at the end of each day, that felt so empty now. Normally, he and his wife would be by the fire, the children curled up at their feet, while he told them of the wonderful strangers he had met that day at the shop.

But not tonight.

Tonight he was alone, and this was not a merry home.

All because Simon Chastain had returned.

He hadn't thought of Simon in years. In fact, he probably hadn't thought of him in at least a decade or two, though perhaps that wasn't entirely true. That day, so long ago, still occasionally haunted his dreams. And every time he passed the old Tremblay place, still abandoned after all these years as no one wanted to take it over for fear of the ghost rumored to be haunting it for the better part of a century, shivers of memories raced up and down his spine, and he always found himself quickening his pace.

Only during those dark times did the thought of Simon Chastain ever pass through his mind.

And never in all his years did he think he'd ever lay eyes upon him again.

41

And yet here he sat, in front of his fire alone, because he had.

And it terrified him.

Everyone in town had seen Simon.

He was unavoidable.

Why did the idiot have to wear his Templar uniform?

It drew an impossible amount of attention in a town so used to strangers traveling through, that any other outfit would have gone unnoticed.

But not a Templar uniform.

And how, after all these years, could he possibly have recognized me?

He pulled at his bright red hair he had been cursed with since birth, answering his own question.

I should have worn a hat.

He grunted.

And I never should have told him to meet me here.

That was the biggest mistake he had made. A panicked decision if there ever was one. In retrospect, he should have sent him on his way, or better yet, proclaimed who he was to the entire town, so he could be arrested and taken away.

But no, he had done the right thing, which never went unpunished in Le Chesnay.

There was a hard knock at the door that sent his heart racing. It came as no surprise, though the inevitability of those three hard raps had left him on edge all evening, from the moment Simon had sought out his parents. And the fact that his expected visitor was now here, in the darkness of the night when no one could see his arrival, had Roland thanking God that he had sent his wife and children to stay with his aunt for the night.

He rose from his chair and drew a deep breath before stepping over to the door and opening it.

"Roland. Sorry to disturb you at this hour."

The apology was insincere, but Roland dared not antagonize the man that now stood before him. "No apology is necessary. It saves me a trip in the morning."

He stepped aside and held out his arm, ushering Gilles Laurent into his small home. He gulped when two of Gilles' men, thugs rather than lawmen, followed, quickly turning the quarters into cramped ones.

"You were planning to see me?"

"Yes. Simon Chastain has returned." Roland's pulse was pounding, and he struggled to sound calm, thankful the fire wasn't enough to reveal the full fear he was certain was written on his face.

Gilles' heavy cane, an affectation only, pounded the floor as if to notify everyone in the room that a lie had just been told. "So you were coming to see me with this most distressing news."

Roland's head bobbed, a little too rapidly. "Of course."

"Why not today?"

"I-I didn't feel it was necessary."

"Why?"

"Because he said he was going to visit his parents. Surely he'd still be there in the morning, and he'd be easier to capture in the light of day."

The cane again pounded the wood floor, twice this time, and Roland flashed back to memories of watching many a good man rapped with it for only the slightest provocation.

And at least several horrendous beatings.

Gilles looked about the small home. "Where are your wife and children?"

Roland flushed. "I sent them to my aunt's."

"Why?"

Roland gulped. "With Simon back, I feared there might be trouble."

"From whom?" A smile spread across Gilles' face. "Me?" His men chuckled, but there was no levity present this night.

"Of course not. From Simon."

"Of course." The cane tapped several times as Gilles rubbed his chin. "I wonder why you invited him back to your home."

"I was shocked. I honestly don't know why I did it. It's been thirty years, after all."

"What did you discuss when you were away from the ears of our good neighbors?"

"Very little, actually. I introduced him to my wife, told him he shouldn't have returned, and that he should be on his way."

"Now why would you say that?"

"Because it's how I felt. No good can come from his return, I'm sure you'll agree."

"Except, perhaps, justice."

Roland's jaw dropped slightly before he snapped it shut.

Justice?

What was Gilles playing at? *He* was the guilty party that had escaped justice all these years, not Simon.

44

Simon was innocent, and only the three of them knew the truth.

"I-I'm not sure what you mean." He glanced at the men, not certain if he should say anything in front of them. "Umm, after all, we both know what happened that day, and it has been all but forgotten by the town. Why drag it back into the open?"

"On the contrary, I don't believe it has been forgotten. It certainly hasn't been by you, and our returned Templar Knight."

"He-he's not a knight. Just a sergeant."

Gilles smiled, switching his cane to his left hand, then drawing his sword. "But he carries a weapon such as this, does he not?"

Roland backed away, raising his hands. "Please, Gilles, I swore I'd say nothing to anyone, and I've kept that promise for over thirty years."

Gilles advanced. "Yet somehow I think your tongue has been loosened slightly with the knowledge that the man you falsely accused is now a powerful warrior."

Roland vigorously shook his head, searching for some means of escape, but the only exit was blocked by Gilles' two men, laughing in the doorway.

The blade thrust forward, piercing his stomach. The pain was sharp and short, not as bad as he would have thought.

Then came the twist.

Agony ripped through him as the blade was withdrawn. He collapsed to his knees as Gilles wiped the blade clean with a cloth Cateline had knit just last year, before sheathing his sword. Roland fell on his side, gripping his stomach as his blood pumped onto the floor, his still-beating heart hastening his demise.

"You-you'll never get away with this."

Gilles smiled, switching his cane back to its preferred hand. "And why shouldn't I? And why should you not want me to? Tonight you died the hero. Simon Chastain, the murderer, returned after all these years. He came to your home. You tried to arrest him for his crimes, and the Templar warrior bested you in a fight, as he should be expected to, and murdered the only other witness to what happened that day so long ago."

Roland wanted to respond, yet couldn't. He was weak now, too much blood lost, blood that now surrounded Gilles' feet. He wanted to damn the man to Hell, but the good Lord would take care of that for him. He just wondered if he would join him in the eternal flames, for having lied all those years ago, and for maintaining the lie, even as a man.

Gilles quickly stepped back, cursing, as he finally noticed he was standing in a pool of his victim's blood. He headed toward the door, taking one last look as Roland's heart pumped its last few beats, the world now dark, the spark of life about to be snuffed out.

"I'm sorry it came to this, my old friend."

I was never your friend.

Roland heard footsteps then the door shut, but not before one final insult to his memory was delivered.

"Now we arrest Simon Chastain for his murder."

Chastain Residence
Le Chesnay, Kingdom of France

Simon's father roared with laughter. "A farmer? If that isn't life coming full circle, I don't know what is. Here you are, born to a poor farmer, you run away and join the Templars, then wind up a farmer anyway. Unbelievable!"

Simon chuckled at his own expense. "If anyone had asked me just this past summer where I thought I would be this winter, I never would have guessed in a million guesses that I'd be on a farm, in Crécy-la-Chapelle, tending livestock and tilling soil, while babysitting a group of children and some wayward women."

His mother leaned forward, patting his knee. "It is a good thing you are doing, son, a very good thing. It is the Lord's work, it is."

Simon sighed, leaning back. "I know it is, yet I find myself unsettled."

His father's eyes narrowed. "And why is that?"

Simon shrugged. "I don't know. I think part of it was the children. They were the first I'd been exposed to since I was a child. It stirred up the old memories. The other is that I've known nothing but fighting the infidel Saracens, and the comradery of the Order, for thirty years. This new life is so…quiet. Peaceful." He sighed. "Different."

"You're not a young man anymore. Perhaps it's time to settle."

He regarded his father. "I think that might be part of it. My body aches now, more than I've ever let my master know, and sometimes the pain is almost unbearable. I could return to the Holy Land and fight the Saracen once more, and perhaps die in battle with our Lord's name on my lips, but my inability to fight as hard as the man beside me might mean their untimely death, and I couldn't live with myself if that were the case. And to go and fight, wanting to die, isn't that just suicide by another name? To die in battle is glorious, and guarantees an eternity at our Lord's side, but only if it is done without intentionally sacrificing oneself merely for the sake of sacrifice. Die to save another? In a heartbeat I'd do it. But just die? For no other reason than to end one's suffering? I can imagine no more cowardly act for a Templar."

His mother wiped a tear away. "Then I think you know what you need to do, my son."

Simon stared at her. "But I don't, Mother. I don't."

"You can't end the pain and torment in battle, without risking your brothers. That means that you can't return to the Holy Land. Yet you wish to continue to be a member of the Order, and to serve God. Perhaps it is time to embrace this new life. Lay down your sword, pick up that plowshare, and live the life the Lord has chosen for you. God has a plan for all of us, and this must be yours. It may not be the life you would have chosen, however, neither was running away and becoming a Templar. God set in motion a series of events that day that not only led you to those men who took you in, but to Sir Marcus and the others. Sir Marcus' destiny led you to the farm, and your doubts led you back to us. And while this may be your childhood home, you know this isn't where you belong anymore. You belong with your brothers, and as much as my heart aches to say it, that farm is your home now, not this drafty old house, or some dusty outpost in the desert."

Simon sat, pondering her words, words that were wise and impartial, spoken by a loving mother to a son she had given up for dead decades ago. For her to push him away was proof enough that they were honest and unselfish thoughts, and because of such, advice that should be heeded.

A heavy knock at the door startled them all, and Simon rose, placing himself between his parents and the ominous announcement at this late hour. He eyed his sword, sitting on the table to his left.

"Open up in the name of the King!"

Simon's heart raced a little faster, King Philip IV no friend to the Templars, and when his name had been invoked over the past several months, it had rarely ended well.

"That's Gilles Laurent," hissed his father, recognizing the voice. "What could he possibly want at this hour?"

But Simon knew. "He wants me."

Simon stepped forward, opening the door to find a slim man, slightly less than average height, sporting clothing far finer than most of those he had so far seen in this humble town, along with four men behind him, swords drawn.

"Simon Chastain?"

Simon bowed slightly. "Gilles Laurent?"

Gilles returned the bow. "So it is true. You have returned."

"I have."

"Why?"

It was a curious question, but not as curious as the question that begged to be asked.

Why were Gilles' men's swords drawn?

"I wanted to see my family, and to clear up any, shall we say, confusion, from when we were children."

"I see. And that is why you saw Roland Villeneuve earlier today? To 'clear up' this confusion?"

"Yes, it is." Simon leaned slightly to his left, making a show of eying Gilles' companions. "And why, might I ask, are your men presenting arms at my parents' home?"

"Because you have been rather busy since you came to town."

Simon tensed, now regretting leaving his sword sheathed, half a dozen paces away. "I don't understand."

"We just came from Roland's home. He's dead."

Simon's mouth opened slightly, his parents gasping behind him. "But I just saw him! He was perfectly healthy. What happened?"

"Why don't you tell me?"

Simon shook his head slightly. "I don't understand."

"A witness saw you enter Roland's home, then saw you leaving a short while later. Do you deny this?"

"Of course not. I've already admitted to visiting with him."

"Good, then this should be easy." Gilles sneered, stepping closer. "This witness, concerned for Roland's safety, entered the home and found Roland dead,

50

gored by a blade to the stomach. Only you could have done such a thing."

Simon's eyes widened. "But that's impossible! When I left, he was perfectly fine. Why, his wife was with him. Cateline! How could I know her name if I hadn't met her?"

Gilles spat. "He likely told you her name, and we haven't found her yet. Did you kill her too? And the children?"

Simon took a step backward, the horror of the accusations unfathomable. "How could you say such a thing? I would never harm women or children."

"Yet we both know that is a lie, don't we?"

Simon shook his head vigorously, jabbing the air between them with a finger. "No! You know that's a lie! You were the one that pushed Christian, not me!"

Gilles laughed. "And the only witness who knew the truth is now dead, dead by your hand. Now, if you were innocent as you claim, then why would you kill him? Is it because *you* are guilty, as I know you to be, and Roland, the only other witness to the events of that day, knew you to be?" He stepped past Simon and approached the terrified parents. "I'm sorry, Mr. and Mrs. Chastain, but your son is guilty of the murder of Christian thirty years ago, and tonight, he is guilty of killing the only other witness who could have proven that fact. Your son is a murderer. Then and now."

Simon's heart broke at the look his father now gave him. "Is this true? Have you been lying to us this entire time?"

Simon reached out for them but they both stepped away, as if repulsed by the thought of his touch. "Of

51

course not! Every word I said was the truth!"

"Then how do you explain Roland's death?"

Simon desperately searched for an answer, quickly hitting upon the only possible explanation. He spun, pointing a finger at Gilles. "You must have done it! Who else could have? You heard I was back in town, and in a desperate attempt to preserve your secret, you killed the only person who could prove my innocence. That has to be it! You did it!"

Gilles smiled slightly. "Yes, that is a perfectly good explanation." He stepped closer. "But you're forgetting one critical thing."

Simon's heart skipped a beat. "What?"

"I have a witness to your crime. You do not." Gilles stepped back, and with the hammering of his cane on the wood, signaled his men to enter. "Take him away!"

Simon didn't bother struggling. He could best these men, he was certain, but they were the law, and killing men who represented the King was never wise. He turned to his parents as shackles were clasped about his wrists. "Mother, father, you have to get word to my master, Sir Marcus de Rancourt in Crécy-la-Chapelle. It's my only hope for justice. Please!"

His father glared at him. "You should never have come back! You're not our son. Our son died thirty years ago, after committing the ultimate sin! And now, you disgrace us by coming here and spreading your lies, only moments after killing the good Roland, who did nothing but tell the truth that day, and live a good, Christian life." He held his sobbing wife tighter against his chest. "Haven't you broken your poor mother's heart enough?" He swept his hand toward the door, turning to Gilles. "Take him away from here. I never want to see this person again!"

"Not to worry, Mr. Chastain, your son will be hanged until dead by morning."

Simon's eyes glistened at his father's words, his stomach in knots as his chest burned, each motion, each expression, each word, another dagger to his heart.

For his father was right, though for the wrong reasons.

He should never have returned.

It was a selfish indulgence.

For if he had simply accepted his fate, and remained on the farm, his parents' lives wouldn't have been shattered once more, and Roland, husband and father, would still be alive.

Though he hadn't wielded the blade that had felled yet another innocent, he might as well have.

And tonight, with Gilles' pronouncement, justice would be as swift as it would have been thirty years ago, and he wouldn't see the light of day, or his master and friend, ever again.

Bailiff's Delegate's Jail
Le Chesnay, Kingdom of France

Simon was freezing. In fact, it was probably the coldest he had felt in his life. The desert was frigid at night after the ground had given up the heat of the day, but there, one usually had shelter or fire, or the shared warmth of one's brothers.

And the starting point of the night was never a chilled body, but an overheated one.

Here, in northern France, in the dead of winter, a winter he had been assured would get far worse before it got better, he was already chilled, and the jail he had been shoved unceremoniously into was barely a cage, the boards making up the walls, spaced so far apart, they were little protection against the wind that howled through. The hardened ground that made up the floor had no heat to give, and the few prisoners he was with were so full of mistrust, each had staked out his own spot, leaving Simon to freeze against one of the empty walls.

Yet his shivering went unnoticed, as his heart was broken. The look on his mother's face as they had dragged him away was seared in his memory, and the hateful words spat at him by his father echoed in his head.

He should never have come back.

Yet how could he have known?

He couldn't. But when he saw the fear in Roland's eyes, he should have immediately turned around, making a point of ensuring everyone who saw him arrive, saw him leave. There would have been talk, then the talk dismissed. His parents would have asked questions, but his return would have eventually been dismissed as rumors, and they would have gone on with their lives. And even if Gilles had visited Roland's residence, Roland would have been able to point to the fact that he had left.

And Roland would still be alive, his wife Cateline would still have a husband, and the children would still have a father, and more importantly, a provider.

Perhaps they should come to the farm.

It wasn't an entirely bad idea, though he doubted they would accept the offer. Everyone and everything they knew was here, and he was merely a distant childhood memory, a stranger known only as a murderer.

He had to get out of this situation before he could help them, regardless, and how he might accomplish that, he didn't know. He had no allies here, not even his parents. There was no chance they would send word to Sir Marcus. They had condemned him, or at least his father had, and that would be the end of it, no matter his mother's wishes.

Though her heartbreak, he feared, was over the realization that her son was indeed a murderer, rather than the sight of an innocent man arrested by the true criminal.

He grabbed the chain clasped around his left ankle and pulled at it yet again to no avail. There was no hope. All of them were chained at the ankle, the other end fastened around a large post in the center of the jail, with no hope of escape. Perhaps if he had time, and they all cooperated, they might remove the post from the frozen ground, but then what? They would run out of town, all still shackled to the same post?

It was laughable.

No, his only hope of escape would be when his chains were unlocked, and that would only happen when they led him to whatever tree they had selected to hang him from. He had no doubt Gilles would put on a show for the entire town to see, to reinforce in their minds that he was still the childhood hero, and that finally he had brought the murderer to justice.

And even if Simon were to protest, to plead with the crowd by revealing the truth, none would believe him.

Why would they?

He was a stranger, and within only hours of arriving, had been arrested for the murder of someone they had lived with for the better part of forty years.

No, he would hang, no matter what was said.

And it devastated him. He didn't fear death. On the contrary, dying this way, an innocent man, would ensure him his path to Heaven, he was certain. It would end his constant pain, and settle the debate that had raged for months on whether life on the farm was for him.

Yet his death would leave his friend, his best friend, Marcus, alone to deal with the women and children, and the two younger squires. Marcus could handle it, of that he had no doubt, but he would handle it without his best friend, and more devastating, would handle it without knowing what had happened to his friend, and why he had never returned.

That was what was crushing him inside, even more

than the pain he had caused his parents, parents he barely knew or remembered.

Marcus and the Order were his life.

And he had never thought it would end this way, in the town he had been born, falsely accused of not one, but two murders, held in a cold prison by his childhood nemesis, only to be hanged then forgotten.

A horse's whinny and the sound of a cart approaching had everyone stirring, no one achieving a deep sleep this night. He stood as several lanterns swung in the dark, the silhouettes of their captors revealed as they neared. The door that held them was unlocked, and the rusted hinges creaked in the night, carried quickly away on the howling wind.

"Chastain! Step forward."

Simon took in a deep breath, unsure of what was happening. "Why? Are you to kill me now, in the dead of night, so there can be no witnesses to your master's treachery?"

"Enough talk," said one, stepping forward with the key. "We're moving you."

Simon's eyes narrowed. "Where?"

The man chuckled, as did the others. "Somewhere justice can be served before your final sentence is carried out."

Simon took a step back. "I don't understand."

"You don't need to." The man took a knee. "Give me your ankle, or I'll have you whipped."

Simon made a decision he feared he might regret. He gave the man his ankle. The key was inserted in the lock and twisted, the chain dropping to the ground.

Then he kneed the man in the face. His jailor cried out, falling backward while gripping his crushed nose, as the others surged inside. Simon kicked the dropped key into the corner, perhaps giving the opportunity for a genuine criminal to escape, but in this moment, he needed to divide the attentions of his captors.

Swords were drawn, and Simon instinctively reached for his own, cursing as he remembered it had been confiscated, along with his trusty dagger. A lantern flew at him and he dodged it, then watched in horror as it shattered on the ground near one of the prisoners, hunched over in the corner. The flames rushed toward the man as the oil splashed across the ground.

Blood-curdling screams tore through the night as the man's clothes caught fire.

Simon lunged forward, punching the nearest of his captors, then booted the other in the groin, neither apparently adept at swordplay. He then rushed to the prisoner he had kicked the key to and yanked it from his hand. The screams continued, and the sound of sizzling flesh was overwhelming as he approached, his hand held up to shield himself from the flames that consumed the prisoner.

Something smacked him on the back of the head and he collapsed, immediately beset upon by his captors. As he struggled to maintain consciousness, he swung an elbow back, catching someone on the chin, the grunt and cry, then freed arm, signaling success. He wrenched loose and scrambled toward the man, his cries now gurgles as the walls burned around them, the flames licking toward the roof, threatening to condemn them all.

Then it all collapsed, a heavy beam overhead falling and pinning Simon to the ground. He struggled to free himself to no avail, his head pounding, his lungs burning from the smoke, when he heard shouts, and smiled. The other men held with him were escaping, the center post weakened now that it was missing its support from above, and he could see them, through the smoke, running together into the darkness.

Then he cried out in horror as the flaming corpse of the third man was dragged behind them, the flickering flames a human torch in the pitch black of the night, and a beacon to their jailers who rushed after them.

He shoved up with his back, one last time, then collapsed, exhausted, as the flames closed in on him.

Somebody laughed behind him, and he twisted his body so he could see who it was.

Gilles.

Simon glared at him. "My master will have his revenge upon you all!"

Gilles stepped forward. "I think not." He swung the heavy cane, mercifully ending the suffering Simon was about to endure.

De Rancourt Residence
Crécy-la-Chapelle, Kingdom of France
AD 1298
One month later

Sir Marcus de Rancourt sat against the southern wall of the barracks, absorbing as much of the warmth from the afternoon sun as he could, though it was of little use. There was simply no comparison to the heat that baked the Holy Land day in and day out.

He missed it.

There was no denying that he too was affected by the melancholy surrounding him. David and Jeremy were hiding it well, though he knew they were having their doubts, fueled by the lack of word from his sergeant and best friend.

It had been over a month since Simon had left, and Marcus was beyond worry. In his haste to appease his friend, no mention of his actual destination was made, except that it was on the opposite side of Paris, about a three days' ride from here.

That could be almost anywhere.

He had already sent word through the local Templar Commandry, messages having gone out across the region seeking word on Simon Chastain, sergeant in the Order, and nothing had come back.

And that was extremely odd.

Simon had promised to check in at the nearest outpost and have word sent back to him, and there was no way he had forgotten to do that. When a week had gone by, he had begun his search, slowly expanding it, but with no success.

It was time to take the next step.

Tanya, the farm's mastiff and his near-constant companion, lifted her head from his lap and stared up at him, snorting, as if she sensed the turmoil raging within. She shoved her snout under his neck, sniffing and licking him until he pushed her away, laughing.

"Enough of that."

He rose and headed for the farmhouse, his decision made. As he approached, he could hear a conversation taking place inside, and he paused, reluctantly eavesdropping.

"He's concerned about Simon, of course," said Lady Joanne.

"As he should be. They're best friends, aren't they?" asked Beatrice.

"Yes, I believe so."

"Is that even possible? A knight and a sergeant? Aren't they of different stations?"

"You're confusing things with the type of nobility and knights we're used to seeing in Paris. The Templars are different. Though the knights are superior in status, they aren't obsessed with wealth and power like ours. And look at us. I consider you my friend, and our stations are quite different."

"This is true, Milady, though perhaps not so much anymore?"

Joanne laughed. "Oh how true, how true!" There was a pause. "I'm not sure what to do about our knight, however. His depression is affecting his men. If Simon doesn't return shortly, I don't know what will happen."

"If he weren't sworn to celibacy, perhaps I could cheer him up. He *is* a handsome devil, isn't he!"

Joanne and Beatrice roared with laughter, and Marcus flushed, now embarrassed at having listened in. He continued toward the front door, clearing his throat loudly. He opened the door and stepped inside.

"Ladies."

He was greeted with stifled giggles and Beatrice's eyes roaming his body.

Joanne pointed toward a chair and Marcus sat. "Sir Marcus. All is well?"

"I am troubled, as I'm sure you've noticed. Simon hasn't returned, and there's been no word from any Templar outpost that they have seen him. I think it is time for me to seek him out."

Joanne frowned. "I thought you didn't know where he lived?"

"I don't know *specifically* where he lived, but I do know that it was about three days' ride from here, to the west of Paris. I'll leave in the morning, and God willing, I will find him."

"And should you not?"

Marcus sighed. "Then I will keep looking."

Joanne leaned forward, patting his hand. "My dear man, have you considered the possibility he may not want to be found?"

Marcus' eyebrows shot up at the suggestion. It was a possibility he most certainly had never considered. He was prepared for his friend to decide to stay with his family, or to leave and actively rejoin the Order, but he had never considered Simon might abandon them, and intentionally hide from him.

"Preposterous."

Joanne nodded slowly. "You know him better than I, so I will bow to your superior wisdom on the matter, but it has been a month with no word, and he never checked in upon his arrival, as he promised to. Is it at all conceivable that within such a short time of arriving, he chose to not check in, if he hadn't already been considering not doing so?"

Marcus stared at her, willing his jaw to remain shut. For she was right. For him to ignore his promise completely, made no sense. He could understand if his friend arrived, spent days or even weeks with old friends and family, and decided that he wanted to remain there, and didn't want to risk anyone coming in search of him, to try and change his mind.

But not the first day. Simon would have immediately checked in. The fact he hadn't, told him there was no Templar outpost in the town he lived in. That was actually helpful, as it narrowed down the list of possible locations, though only slightly. And if he had found himself in his hometown, with no place to check in, he would certainly have done so the very next day, leaving little time for him to abandon decades of loyalty.

There was simply no way.

That meant something else must be at play.

And perhaps it was as Lady Joanne said. Perhaps he had never intended on coming back.

Marcus grunted, dismissing the idea. "I know my sergeant, and there is no way he would do as you say."

"Then what do you think has happened?"

Marcus frowned. "I think something has happened to him." He rose. "And I intend to find out what."

Joanne stood. "You should take the squires with you. If something happened to Simon, then the same could happen to you."

Marcus dismissed the suggestion. "No, they'll remain here with you. You and the children need their protection more than I do." He patted Tanya on the head. "I'll take the dog with me. She's proven useful in a fight."

Joanne frowned, staring at the dog. "If only she could wield a sword."

Marcus chuckled. "You'd be surprised what a good snarl and a mouthful of teeth can do to a man's courage."

Joanne nodded. "True. Then it is settled. You're leaving in the morning. We'll prepare some food for your journey, and I'm sure your squires will prepare your horse." She stepped forward, taking his hands in hers. "And be sure to allot some time for saying goodbye to the children. They do adore you so, and this will sadden them greatly, even more so should you leave with merely a wave of the hand."

Marcus stared down at Joanne with a smile. "You barely know me, yet I feel as if we have been close for years."

"That's because we're family, and family is always connected, no matter how far."

He sighed. "You are right, of course. I shall spend the evening with the children." He let go of her hands, stepping back toward the door. "But now I must inform my other two children of my plan."

"I resent that!"

Marcus chuckled at Jeremy's voice through the door. "What have I said about listening in on other people's conversations?"

"Nothing that I recall. And you were doing it only moments ago."

Beatrice gasped and blushed, Marcus doing the same as he averted his gaze.

Joanne simply laughed. "How wonderful! Sir Marcus, I'm sure my chambermaid's services are still available should you wish to avail yourself of them!"

Beatrice lifted her dress suggestively several inches, revealing a pair of ankles, sending Marcus out of the house in a hail of delighted giggles, nearly bowling over David and Jeremy, their ears evidently pressed against the door only moments before.

He glared at their snickers, and they tried to stifle them to no avail, scampering after him as he marched up the hill toward their barracks. "I'm leaving in the morning. Prepare my horse for a three-day journey. See Beatrice for provisions."

"Yes, sir," replied David. "But do you think it's wise to go alone?"

Marcus stopped and turned to face them, pointing at the home. "The women and children are far more important than my life. Remember that."

David and Jeremy both bowed their heads. "Yes, sir."

He resumed his climb. "I'll be taking Tanya with me. She's protection enough." He paused, a thought occurring to him as the squires caught up. "I wonder…" He snapped his fingers, turning to Jeremy. "Take a horse to our headquarters in Paris at once. Ask them if they have any records on Simon, and if those records include a hometown. We might get lucky."

Jeremy bounced in place. "Right away, sir!" He sprinted for the stables.

"And if you're not back before I leave, send word to the Commandry in Versailles. I'll get the message there!"

"Yes, sir!" replied Jeremy from inside, his voice echoing, the horses whinnying at the disturbance.

David followed his master to the barracks. "How long should we wait before we come looking for you?"

Marcus glanced at him. "I'll be back, don't worry."

"We thought the same of Simon."

"I have no doubts about staying on the farm."

David regarded him. "With all due respect, we both know that isn't true. However, we also both know that you swore an oath to protect those children, and you are a man of your word, therefore I have no doubt you will keep it. What I mean is, so is Simon. And he swore that same oath. He would never break it without your blessing."

Marcus frowned. "Your point?"

"My point is, something happened to him, something bad. And if it can happen to him, it can happen to you. So I ask again, at what point should I begin to worry?"

Marcus grunted. "You will hear from me at least once a week. If you don't, send word to the Order, and let them deal with it. Your duty is to the women and children."

David frowned, clearly not pleased with his orders, but nodded. "Very well."

They both watched through the empty doorway as

Jeremy charged down the hill, toward the road leading through town then on to Paris. He'd be there before nightfall, and probably have his answer by morning. If God were on their side, Marcus might encounter him on his journey tomorrow, and worst case, he'd get the answer, or lack thereof, when he reached the Commandry in Versailles.

And if the answer was that the Order knew not where Simon was born, then he feared it would be like searching for a needle in a haystack.

And perhaps it might be a needle that didn't want to be found.

Templar Commandry
Versailles, Kingdom of France
Three Days Later

God apparently hadn't been on their side, though Marcus was certain it was because He had more important things to do than reuniting him with Jeremy on the road to Paris. The search of the records had evidently taken longer than he had hoped. It was now three days since Jeremy had been dispatched, and any response that he had requested would have been sent by messenger, and have likely arrived here within less than a day.

Though that didn't necessarily mean he'd be content with the response.

He dismounted in front of the small though impressive structure, the flag of the Order fluttering in the chilly breeze signaling the presence of Templars amidst the town. With outposts and depots, along with commandries spread across Christendom, a Templar was never far from friends or supplies, and seeing the flag, and his brothers coming and going, brought him a comfort he hadn't realized he had been yearning for.

Thirty years surrounded by white, black, and brown tunics, with red crosses emblazoned in the middle, was deeply missed.

He tied up his horse and entered, a brown-shirted squire holding open the door for him. "Welcome, Milord."

Marcus acknowledged the lad with a nod of his

head, then stepped deeper into the structure, an elderly man, wearing the bright white tunic of a knight, evidently retired to light duty, sat behind a desk. He looked up at the new arrival, a long scar marring his face from forehead to chin, one eye a dull gray.

Obviously a man of honor.

"I am Sir Marcus de Rancourt."

The man rose. "And I am Sir Piers de Vichiers." He bowed his head, Marcus doing the same, then picked up a folded piece of paper from his desk. "I have a message for you."

Marcus smiled, his heart racing a little faster as he took the paper. "Thank you."

"Can we be of any further service?"

Marcus nodded as he cracked the seal, unfolding the page. "Yes, if you could have my horse exchanged for a fresh one, and supplies for two days' ride."

Piers snapped his fingers and a young boy ran over. "A new horse for Sir Marcus, and two days' provisions."

The boy bowed deeply, then rushed out the front door as Marcus read the letter from Jeremy.

And smiled.

"Le Chesnay. Have you heard of it?"

Piers nodded. "Yes. About an hours' ride from here, to the north. Just follow the main road out of here and you can't miss it. But be careful. We've had reports of highwaymen in the area."

"Really? Have they disturbed any in our Order?"

Piers shook his head. "Not that I've heard, but one can always be the first."

Marcus chuckled. "With the way my luck has been lately, it's liable to be me."

Piers wagged a finger with a smile. "Now, now, we shouldn't be believing in luck as good Christians."

Marcus laughed. "You are right of course. I think a quick stop in the church is in order. I do have a few sins to confess."

Piers sighed, sitting back in his chair with the wince of old age. "I find lately I have to go every day, my feelings of self-pity leading me astray far too often."

Marcus sat across from him as the sounds of his horse being tended to could be heard outside. "I too am guilty of this." He nodded toward the scar. "Where, might I ask, did you acquire that token?"

"Outside La Roche-Guillaume."

"Antioch." Marcus patted his left shoulder, still slightly tender at times. "I was there as well. Took an arrow to my shoulder."

Piers sighed. "Warriors were never meant to grow old. We were meant to die in battle, in glorious service to our Lord Jesus Christ. Instead, I survive a blow, that if it were but an inch closer, would have killed me, and now am no longer fit for battle, but still fit to administer the mighty business of the Order." He grunted. "With all this complaining, I think I'll be joining you for confession."

Marcus chuckled. "I too have been relegated to a life of boredom, though for entirely different reasons. I have the option of giving it up, and returning to fight, but I swore an oath, and I dare not break it."

Piers nodded. "Then your destiny is set, my friend. If an oath has been sworn, only he you swore it to can free you from it."

Marcus thought of his dead sister, and wondered how an oath sworn to her spirit could ever be forgiven. "I fear that isn't possible."

Piers frowned. "Then you must make peace with it, and embrace it." He exhaled loudly. "As must I."

The young boy rushed in. "Your horse is ready, Milord."

Marcus nodded at the boy then rose, Piers doing the same. "I thank you for your service, Sir Piers."

"And I yours, Sir Marcus." He stepped around his desk, holding an arm out toward the door. "Shall we confess our sins before you continue on your journey?"

Marcus thought of what might have happened to Simon, and decided a cleansed soul was a wise precaution. "Lead the way, my friend."

Approaching Le Chesnay, Kingdom of France

Marcus rode in silence, his horse at a good but reasonable pace, as there was no point in exhausting the beast should he need some speed out of her. And with highwaymen possibly on the route, and Simon more important than heroics, he'd likely effect a hasty escape, rather than take on an unknown number.

Tanya growled.

"What is it, girl?"

Tanya stopped, staring into the trees to their right, then her head swung to look at the other side. Marcus brought the horse to a halt and listened, hearing nothing at first, then some rustling in the trees.

On both sides of the road.

Highwaymen.

It was most likely that. An animal on one side of the road, making noise as it moved through the trees was a possibility, though both sides, in multiple locations, told him it was not fauna he had to worry about, but humans up to no good.

He spotted a shadow, the silhouette of a man, eliminating any doubt.

He inhaled loudly, thrusting his chest out, his arms at his sides as he urged the horse forward at a slow walk, turning to his left then his right in his saddle, making sure anyone who had eyes on him could see his white surcoat and red cross.

"I warn you now! I am a Templar Knight, which means I have no money, but I do have a sword that has removed the heads of many a Saracen." He smiled. "Should any of you wish to join them in Hell, I'll be more than happy to oblige."

The only response was harsh whispers, clearly a debate occurring on either side of the road, then silence.

"Have a good day, gentlemen."

Marcus urged his horse forward a little faster, in case the brigands changed their minds, but was soon on the outskirts of the town of Le Chesnay, where his sergeant and best friend had been hatched so long ago. He had to admit he was surprised, the town clearly busy with travelers, its position less than half a day from Paris, ideal for the weary to rest for a night, then face the travails of the capital fresh.

Though it was clear Templars evidently didn't frequent here, if the stares he was receiving were any indication.

But there was something more in the eyes.

Fear, laced with anger.

He recognized it well from the stares of conquered Saracens.

These people were scared of him, and angry as well.

Yet it couldn't be him specifically, since none knew who he was.

That meant it was his Templar markings.

These people were scared of him as a Templar, not Sir Marcus de Rancourt. And as they should have no reason to fear Templars in general, he had to assume there was some specific reason.

And it had to be Simon.

If Simon had indeed arrived here a month ago, as he suspected, then these people would have seen him, as this was the only road through the town. Did he receive the same greeting? And was the anger acted upon? Simon was a tremendous warrior, but some numbers were simply too overwhelming.

He tossed his surcoat clear of the hilt of his sword, just in case, the revealing of it turning much of the anger to mere fear.

These people attacked no one.

Yet the anger had been there, which implied a negative experience with a Templar at some point in the near past.

And he prayed it wasn't Simon, though he couldn't imagine it would be. Simon was the best man he knew. Pious, humble, and the defender of innocents like this. None should ever fear him, unless they intended harm to innocent souls.

He spotted an old woman with neither fear nor anger in her eyes, and approached her. "Good day to you."

She nodded. "And to you. Can I be of service?"

"I'm looking for the Chastain family."

This got a reaction from those within earshot, though the old woman merely nodded, as if she knew his business. "Keep going the way you've been, until you're out of town. They have a farm on the left, just after the small bridge. You can't miss it."

Marcus bowed in his saddle. "Thank you, Milady."

She cackled, the others joining in. "I don't know if I've ever been called that."

"You've been called a lot worse, I can assure you!" cried another woman nearby.

74

The entire row of vendors roared with laughter, friendly insults exchanged among those manning the stalls. Marcus smiled, pleased the fear and anger were gone, and continued through the town, taking in everything with his trained eye. If something had happened to Simon here, he didn't want to risk missing anything. By the time he had reached the edge of the town, he had only noticed one thing out of the ordinary.

A burned-out building next to the Bailiff's Delegate's office. What it had once been, he couldn't be sure, but the fact blackened remains were still present among the collapsed walls, suggested to him that those housed there were not only of no importance to the townsfolk, but were left there as a message to someone.

A jail?

It was possible. Larger towns were known to have their own jails while prisoners awaited trial or transport, yet he had never heard of bodies left to decay after one burned down.

Then again, he could honestly say he had never heard of one burning.

He crossed a small bridge and spotted a rundown farm to his left, frowning at the sight. It was clear it wasn't well tended, which suggested, if this was Simon's old home, his family had fallen on hard times.

Why hasn't his brother taken over?

The wisp of a fire rose from the chimney, erasing any suggestion that the farm had been abandoned, but Marcus saw no evidence of Simon's horse here, nor in the barn to the left.

Where are you, my old friend?

He rode up to the house and dismounted, tying up his horse. He pointed at the ground, ordering Tanya to stay, then, stepping onto the porch, he knocked firmly, though gently, so as not to startle anyone who might be inside. Shuffling gave way to the creak of the door, an old man and woman standing on the other side.

With fear in their eyes.

"Are you Mr. and Mrs. Chastain? Parents to Simon?"

Anger replaced the fear in the man's eyes, though tears joined the fear in the woman's.

"We are. Are you Sir Marcus de Rancourt?"

It was Marcus' turn to be taken aback, though it was quickly replaced with elation, for there was only one way they could know his name.

Simon had arrived safely.

He bowed deeply to the parents of the best friend he had ever known. "I am."

"Then we have you to blame for our son's death."

Chastain Residence
Le Chesnay, Kingdom of France

Marcus sat across from Simon's parents, surprised at having been invited inside and offered a hot tisane by the family's matriarch, after what he had just heard. To be accused of being responsible for their son's death had been a shock, yet any anger he sensed didn't seem directed at him, and Tanya hadn't even emitted so much as a growl, leaving Marcus confident there was no ill will directed at him.

"Please, tell me, what happened to Simon?"

Mrs. Chastain bit down on her finger, stifling what obviously were painful memories, leaving her husband to reply. "He arrived about a month ago, and before the night was through, he had murdered a man he knew as a child, been arrested, then died in a fire while trying to escape."

Marcus leaned back, his mouth agape. It was outrageous. It was unfathomable. It was...

He was at a loss for words, even in his own mind. To think that Simon was capable of any of these things was absolute insanity, absolute balderdash.

He drew a quick breath, closing his mouth. "I must admit, I find this all very hard to believe."

"If you knew his past, you wouldn't."

Marcus' eyebrows shot up. "His past? I don't understand."

"I thought you were his master. His friend for over twenty years. He didn't tell you?"

77

Marcus frowned. "Simon told me everything, except that which related to his youth. All I know is that he left home at a young age, and has a brother. That's all."

"*Had* a brother. He's responsible for *his* death too."

Marcus' eyes narrowed. "My sergeant now stands accused of two deaths. Someone a month ago, and his own brother."

"Three."

Marcus' eyes widened once again. "Three? Perhaps you should explain from the beginning."

The old man grumbled, clearly not pleased to reveal what he was about to, but Marcus had found his bearing and uniform made many speak who didn't want to, and he wasn't about to let the man off the hook. He needed to know why his best friend was dead, then find some private place to let escape the grief that overwhelmed him.

For it did.

Every fiber of his being was in agony with the confirmation of his worst fears. His best friend was dead, accused of murder, and if guilty, as Simon's own parents seemed convinced, was condemned to burn in Hell for eternity.

"Before our son ran away, he killed a boy. In a fit of anger, he beat him, then pushed him into the river. The boy fell through the ice and drowned. Simon ran away, and never returned. Until a month ago."

Marcus shook his head. "I never knew." He thought of how his friend seemed haunted by some past memory every time the boys roughhoused. It had to be why. And the fact he was troubled by it,

78

suggested guilt. "What was the boy's name?"

"Christian Samuel."

"And how do you know Simon did it?"

The old man stared at him. "Excuse me?"

"Well, if Simon pushed Christian into the river, then ran away, how do you know what happened?"

"There were witnesses."

Marcus' head bobbed slowly. "Who?"

"Two of his friends. One, Gilles Laurent, the Bailiff's Delegate's son, was there. He fought my boy, trying to stop him from getting away, but failed."

"You said witnesses?"

"The other was Roland Villeneuve. The man my son murdered a month ago, only moments after arriving in town."

Marcus folded his arms, considering what he had just heard. "So, four boys are out playing. An altercation occurs. One dies in the river." He paused his summation. "Did they find the body?"

Mr. Chastain shook his head. "Never."

Mrs. Chastain finally spoke. "Poor Mrs. Samuel. I fear she still believes he's alive, lost somewhere."

Marcus acknowledged her entry into the conversation with a brief smile, but returned to the facts. "After this altercation, this Gilles boy fights with Simon, Simon runs away, never to return, and Gilles, along with Roland, inform everyone of what transpired."

"It appears you have a firm grasp of the situation."

"Were you there for this revelation?"

"Much to our humiliation. It occurred on a Sunday, and most of the town was still gathered.

Everyone got to hear what my son had done."

Marcus sighed. "And then, a month ago, Simon arrives in town, immediately kills one of the witnesses to what transpired that day, then what? Comes here?"

"Yes."

"Did he tell you of the murder?"

"Of course not. In fact, he denied he killed Christian all those years ago."

Marcus smiled slightly. Everything he had heard so far completely contradicted everything he knew about his friend, though what one was as a child often bore no resemblance to the man one became, and childhood transgressions could in fact positively influence the future adult.

But now, a doubt had been introduced. Simon claimed he was innocent. Yet did any of that matter now? Simon was dead. Would clearing his good name of a childhood crime be worth the pain that could be stirred up by asking questions?

Yet none of that explained the murder of Roland, the more pressing matter.

"How did Simon even find Roland? He hadn't seen the man in over thirty years. How could he possibly have found him?"

"Roland always had rather distinctive red hair. Apparently, Simon saw him in the street when he arrived, asked if he was Roland, then the two met in Roland's house shortly after. It was at this time that he murdered him."

Marcus slowly shook his head. He could believe that something happened when Simon was a boy. Children didn't understand the consequences of their actions at times. But for the Simon he knew to murder a man in cold blood within moments of seeing him for the first time in thirty years, made no sense.

Unless...

"Could Roland have actually pushed Christian in the river?"

Mr. Chastain's eyes widened briefly. "No."

"You sound certain."

"I am. My boy did it, though he claims otherwise."

Marcus bit his tongue, not wanting to let loose his anger over this man not supporting his son. "Did Simon say who did it?"

Mr. Chastain nodded but said nothing, fear entering his visage, his wife clearly terrified.

"Please, sir, I must know."

The old man sighed loudly. "He claimed Gilles did it."

"The Bailiff's Delegate's son."

"Yes."

"And why is this not believable?"

"Because Roland said it wasn't so, and my son ran away. If that's not the mark of a guilty man, I don't know what is."

Marcus decided not to press the matter. "Your son, you said he died the same night he was arrested."

"Yes."

"Who arrested him?"

"The Bailiff's Delegate and his men."

Marcus chewed his cheek for a moment. "I assume it's not the same Bailiff's Delegate from thirty years ago?"

A burst of air erupted from Mr. Chastain. "I wish! Mr. Laurent was an honorable man. A good man. But his son! Bah! Don't get me started."

Marcus leaned forward. "I don't understand."

"Gilles Laurent is now the Bailiff's Delegate. He was granted his father's position after he died."

Marcus leaned back, letting out a slow breath. "So the boy who accused Simon of murder thirty years ago, also accused him a month ago, and made the arrest."

"Yes."

Marcus shook his head in disbelief. "How do they know Simon killed him, besides the fact that he visited him?"

"They had a witness, apparently. Somebody saw him go inside with Roland, then leave a short while later, apparently agitated or something. The witness was concerned, so went inside, and found Roland on the floor, dead from a stab wound. The type made by a sword." The man nodded toward Marcus', sitting on the floor at his side.

"Who was the witness?"

"How should I know?"

Mrs. Chastain raised a shaking finger. "I heard it was one of Gilles' men."

Marcus snorted. "You're telling me that Simon stood accused of murder by one of Gilles Laurent's men, and that was believed?"

"In this town, one doesn't question anything Gilles Laurent or one of his men says."

"Why?"

The fear returned to both their faces, and they remained silent.

"Very well. You said Simon died trying to escape.

How?"

"There was a fire at the jail."

Marcus' eyebrows popped. "So this town does have a jail. Do you have a big enough problem that you couldn't let Paris deal with it?"

Mr. Chastain stared at the floor. "It was built a couple of years ago by Gilles, with permission from the Bailiff. There's been a problem with, umm, crime."

Mrs. Chastain's eyes were like daggers, stabbing at her husband.

Marcus turned to her. "What's wrong?"

She vehemently shook her head. "I, umm, can't say."

Mr. Chastain leaned forward, clasping his hands together. "Please don't ask us any more questions. We've lost enough already." He glanced at his wife as if he feared she might be next.

Marcus decided there was no point in pressing the matter. He had heard enough for his suspicions to be raised, and these people had been through enough. "Very well. I do, however, want to visit your son's grave and pay my respects. Where is he buried?"

Shame replaced the fear, and Mr. Chastain's eyes drifted to the floor. "You'll have to ask Gilles."

Marcus' jaw nearly dropped. "Why? You don't know?"

"He never claimed the body!" cried Mrs. Chastain, sobbing. "You heartless bastard!"

Mr. Chastain's head dipped between his knees and his shoulders shook, but he said nothing.

Marcus rose. "I'll go see him in the morning."

Mrs. Chastain leaped to her feet. "I'm going with

83

you!"

Her husband stared up at her. "You absolutely are not!"

"He's our son! I don't care what they say he did, he's my boy, and I want him buried properly!"

Mr. Chastain threw his hands up in the air in exasperation. "Fine, woman, if it will shut you up, *I'll* go and claim the body. But you're staying here!"

His wife returned to her chair, saying nothing.

Mr. Chastain turned to Marcus. "I'll go with you in the morning, just please don't make any trouble for us by asking too many questions. Around these parts, it can get one hurt." He stared into Marcus' eyes. "Or worse."

THE SERGEANT'S SECRET

Bailiff's Delegate's Office
Le Chesnay, Kingdom of France

"What happened?"

The Bailiff's Delegate, Gilles Laurent, stared at Marcus from behind an impressive desk that had seen better days, though its solid construction meant it would see many more. "And who are you again? His master?"

"As I said, I am Sir Marcus de Rancourt, member of the Knights Templar. Simon Chastain was my sergeant and my friend for over twenty years."

Gilles grunted. "You should choose better friends." His men, standing about the room, chuckled. They were clearly there to intimidate, though it was only working on the elderly Chastain. "And you, Mr. Chastain, why after all this time do you finally come to claim the body of your disgraced son?" He threw a hand toward Marcus. "Is it because of him?"

Chastain kept his head bowed, his eyes on the floor, his hat clasped in both hands. "I do it for my wife. She grieves for her son."

"And you don't?"

"Yes, I do, but women are more delicate."

Marcus put an end to the intimidation. "You were about to tell me what happened?"

"Was I?" Gilles regarded Marcus, as if trying to determine who would win in a fight. He pursed his lips, apparently deciding it wasn't worth the risk. "He died trying to escape."

"I find that hard to believe."

"Well, you didn't apparently know him very well. Though I'll give you this. We were going to transfer your sergeant when he attacked my men. A lantern was knocked loose and a fire started. Your sergeant died trying to save the other men."

Marcus' chest tightened. *That* was the Simon he knew. *That* was the fitting end for a career of service.

And it meant his friend was definitely dead.

"Where was he buried?"

Gilles laughed. "Buried? He wasn't buried! Why should the Crown pay for that when he has family here?"

Marcus leaped from his chair as the realization hit him of what was really being said. He jabbed a finger toward the burned-out building next door. "Are you telling me that the body I saw outside is my sergeant?"

"A rather fitting end for a man responsible for two murders, thirty years apart, don't you think? I can assure you, the example he is setting, lying there in disgrace, will save lives in the long run."

Marcus stormed from the office and jumped from the porch onto the frozen ground, making for the remains of the jail, his eyes quickly finding the body of his friend, covered with a light dusting of snow. He held out a hand toward Simon's father as he exited the office. "Mr. Chastain, please remain there, you shouldn't see this. In fact, go home, and I will deal with this."

The old man nodded gratefully and struggled down the two steps to the road. He climbed onto his cart and unlocked the brake, flicking his reins, the horse whinnying then advancing. Chastain turned them around to head back to the farm, and Marcus' heart broke as the elderly man stole a glance at the remains of his son, his face one of shocked horror at the sight.

Why did you look?

Yet he couldn't fault the man. He would have done the same.

He watched the old man depart, then stepped into the wreckage, tossing aside several boards as the townsfolk gathered and watched the spectacle.

It enraged him.

But he held his tongue.

Finally clear of any debris, Marcus made the sign of the cross over his friend's body, his eyes closed as he said a silent prayer.

Then he opened them, and stifled a gasp.

The body at his feet had a horribly warped spine.

The body at his feet could never have swung a sword.

The body at his feet was not his friend.

He was about to demand an explanation when he remembered the pleas of his friend's parents. They were scared of Gilles Laurent for some reason, and didn't want any trouble.

Marcus turned, glaring at the crowd, surprised at what he saw. These people weren't giddy at his misery, they weren't excited to see a Templar Knight grieve over a friend's body.

They were scared.

Or worse, bereft of any feelings.

He knew the expression. He had seen it in many a siege.

These people were defeated.

Marcus stepped from the remains of the structure and onto the road. He mounted his horse then turned to Gilles. "I'll be back for the body after I've made proper arrangements."

Gilles bowed his head slightly. "As you wish. He's not going anywhere."

Marcus bit his tongue and urged his horse forward, whistling at Tanya to follow, the good girl growling at Gilles' disrespect. As he left the town, he continued to watch the people who lived here, and but for the odd smile plastered on for a customer, he sensed no joy, no happiness, no optimism.

This was a town under siege.

And it had to be related to Gilles Laurent.

The question was how? Surely if enough people complained to the Bailiff, or to the King's Court, he would be removed from his post.

But that took bravery, and the average person lacked it. The average person kept their head down, minded their own business, and simply tried to survive.

These were peasants, not knights.

Not like him.

And as a knight, it was his duty to discover the truth.

And the truth was that the body was not his friend's.

That meant he hadn't died in the fire as Gilles claimed.

What Marcus couldn't understand was why Gilles would lie about such a thing. Why fake Simon's death? Gilles was the law, he had a witness, and apparently, a town convinced that Simon had committed a murder thirty years ago as well.

Few would object to a good hanging under those circumstances.

So why pretend that the body lying in the fire was that of Simon?

It made no sense.

But one thing did.

Simon was alive. Of that, he was certain.

The question was where.

He crossed the bridge and rode onto the Chastain property, the old man coming from the barn, evidently having just finished unhitching his horse. Marcus stopped him before they entered the house.

"I have news that may distress you."

Chastain stared up at him. "I can't imagine any that could be worse than what we have already suffered."

Marcus drew a slow breath. "The body we saw today is not that of your son."

Chastain's jaw dropped as he took a step back. "What are you saying? How can you know?"

"His spine was bent."

The old man sighed. "I couldn't see. Thankfully, my eyesight isn't what it once was. The good Lord mercifully spared me from seeing my son's body clearly."

"And I assure you, my good man, that the body you saw wasn't your son."

"But how can you know? A bent spine? What does that mean? Maybe it simply melted in the fire like metal in a forge?"

Marcus shook his head. "I'm afraid it doesn't work

that way. I've seen many burned bodies in my lifetime, and bone doesn't bend in fire."

Chastain scratched his chin, his free hand twisted behind him, feeling his spine. "But how could you know his spine wasn't bent without seeing it?"

"Because there is no way that man could stand straight."

Chastain sighed. "I haven't seen my boy in so long, I couldn't tell you whether he stood straight or not."

"Well, sir, I have, and I assure you he did."

"Then what are you saying? That that isn't my boy?"

"There is no possible way it is."

"Then who is it?"

Marcus shrugged. "I don't know. Perhaps another prisoner."

"But how could they make such a mistake?"

Marcus shook his head. "I don't think they did. I think we were lied to."

"But why?"

"I'm not sure, but for some reason, they want us to think Simon is dead."

"He was going to hang anyway! Why keep him alive?"

"I don't know." Marcus regarded Chastain. "Can *you* think of any reason?"

Chastain stared at him for a moment, his head slowly shaking, then he shrugged. "A lot of people were angry when Christian died. The entire town was ready to lynch my son. Perhaps someone wants him to face a different kind of justice."

Marcus frowned. "This is possible, though if it is, it

can't be Gilles."

"Why not?"

"Because he would have nothing to gain by it. A quick death would be in his best interest."

"But why? Maybe he wants Simon to suffer so he can claim it as payback for Christian and Roland's deaths. It would perhaps please the families."

Marcus shook his head. "You're forgetting one thing."

"What?"

"If that were the purpose, a month has passed. Surely he would have told everyone by now what he had done." Marcus sighed. "No, I think something else is going on here, and perhaps our most likely suspect actually has nothing to do with it at all."

"You mean maybe he doesn't know the body isn't Simon's?"

"Perhaps. One of his men could have lied to him. Unless you knew what you were looking at, few would be able to tell it wasn't him."

"Then you're saying someone out there has my boy, for some unknown reason, and is doing God only knows what to him?"

Marcus frowned, his stomach sick from the thought. "I fear so."

"Then what are you going to do? You have to find him!"

Marcus stared grimly at the man. "I'm not sure where to begin, but I assure you, I will do everything within my power to bring your son back to you."

Chastain frowned. "So he can face the noose once again."

91

Unknown Location
Kingdom of France

Simon howled in pain. There was no shame in it. Even the strongest of men would. He had held it in at first, refusing to give his torturers the satisfaction, yet it didn't take long for him to realize he was doing nothing to them, and everything to himself.

For his silence only encouraged them to twist the knobs a little further, to crack the whips a little harder, to crank the wheels a little faster.

Causing him even more pain.

But if he held out just the right amount, then gave in to the pain, they backed off that much sooner, their job done.

Unfortunately, it had taken him almost a week to figure that out.

At least he assumed it was a week. He hadn't seen the light of day since he had arrived here, and in fact, wasn't certain how he had gotten here. The last thing he remembered was Gilles hitting him with the cane amidst the fire, then waking up in a filthy, rat-infested, excrement-filled cell.

Followed by the torture sessions, hours in length, yet never truly enough to do any serious damage.

Which was odd.

He had no doubt Gilles was behind this, though to what end, he wasn't sure. It simply made no sense. Gilles wanted him dead. There could be no doubt in that. He had murdered poor Roland then pinned the murder on him, gleefully proclaiming he'd be dead by the morning.

So why keep him alive?

They had come that night to take him somewhere, likely here, and his resistance and the fire hadn't changed those plans. But those plans made no sense, unless he was being sent for a trial elsewhere.

And if that were the case, there was no need for the torture he now underwent.

For not a single question had been asked of him since he arrived.

He would be taken from his cell, tortured in near silence, then returned. At some point during the day, food and water would be delivered, enough to keep him barely alive, then nothing. He had no human interaction whatsoever beyond pleading with whoever brought his food to get word to Marcus, though there was never a response.

The ratchet clicked to his right, and his limbs stretched on the rack just a little further, enough to elicit yet another scream of agony, and the sensation that just one more turn would dislocate his arms, or worse, his legs.

This was further than they had ever gone before, and he had the distinct impression his torturers were getting bored.

Another sign there was no purpose to this.

"One more?" asked the operator.

Simon was about to answer when he heard footsteps behind him. He couldn't see who had been asked the question, but he had a sense he had been there the entire time, on many occasions. Simon never heard him speak a word, apparently all his instructions non-verbal, as was today's.

"Very well."

A lever was pulled, releasing the ratchet mechanism, and suddenly his arms and legs loosened, relief washing over his body. He cried out in exquisite reprieve, an orgasmic rush leaving him weeping without shame at the mercy once again shown him.

And again leaving him mired in confusion.

He was carried between two guards back to his cell then tossed inside, the heavy metal door slamming behind him as he collapsed on the floor strewn with clumped up, filthy hay, and God only knew what other grime left behind by countless others.

The footsteps of his guards receded, and he was once again left in the deafening solitude that had become the majority of his days. He struggled to the corner he had made into his own, laying his head on a pile of the cleanest hay he could manage, then closed his eyes, praying for the sweet relief of sleep as the temporary ecstasy of his torture ending wore off, replaced by the aching pain of muscles and bones stretched beyond their limits.

And a furious headache.

What he would give for some wine now to deaden the pain.

Surely, the good Lord would forgive me for the indulgence.

His eyes burned with self-pity when the door outside clanged open, signaling either the beginning of another torture session, or the delivery of his daily meal.

The small panel at the bottom of the door opened and he forced himself forward, a plate and cup pushed through. He opened his mouth to beg once again for a message to be delivered, but he didn't bother.

It was no use.

Marcus would never find out what had happened to him, and would forever assume his trusted sergeant had abandoned his duties, and broken his oath.

And it crushed him.

"Is it true you're a Templar?"

It was the sweetest sound he had heard in weeks. A woman, a young woman, and the first words spoken to him in so long, he almost forgot to respond.

"Yes." He struggled closer to the door. "Where am I?"

"In La Conciergerie Prison."

The news was actually slightly comforting, for he knew of this place, and it was in Paris, where the Templar headquarters for the entire kingdom resided. "You must get word to my master, Sir Marcus de Rancourt. Just tell any Templar, or go to the headquarters. They'll be able to find him."

There was a pause, then an extra piece of bread rolled through the hole, something that had never happened before. "I will try, though I doubt there is anything that can be done. Whoever put you here must truly hate you."

Simon nodded in the near complete darkness. "You *must* try. Freeing me isn't of importance. It is letting my master know what happened that is, for I fear I shall die soon, and I don't want him thinking I abandoned my oath to him."

The small opening snapped shut, leaving him once again in complete darkness.

But with a renewed sense of hope that though he

might die, his master and friend would know the truth.

Simone Thibault Residence
Paris, Kingdom of France

Sabine hated coming here. Abhorred it. The woman who lived here was one of the richest women she knew that wasn't nobility, though she knew none of the aristocracy herself. Simone Thibault was pure evil, as far as Sabine was concerned, but she was also a woman who paid for information, and today she had some that might prove valuable.

For the Templars were rich.

Not the individuals. They were sworn to poverty. But the Order was wealthier than most kings, and they would probably pay dearly for word of one of their own locked away in La Conciergerie Prison.

Yet she had no idea how to parlay her knowledge into coin.

But Thibault would.

She knocked on the door, her heart hammering, even more so the moment it opened, revealing the behemoth of a man that protected the unpopular Thibault.

"Enzo. Good to see you once again."

He nodded. "And you. What's your business?"

"I have information that I believe your mistress will find very valuable."

"Why don't you tell it to me, and I'll decide."

Sabine smiled. "You know that's not how it works."

Enzo grunted then stepped aside. She entered the

finest home her shadow had ever graced, then followed Enzo up the stairs and down a long hall that ended in Thibault's office. He knocked twice then opened the door.

"Sabine Bisset to see you, madam."

"Sabine! Come in, young one!"

The excited utterance was pure fiction. When Thibault wanted to, she could charm anyone. It was how she lured in her victims. But once her claws were buried deep within one's wallet and future prospects, she would turn vicious if her terms weren't followed to the letter.

Sabine entered the office, forcing a smile as her entire body continued to shake. "Mrs. Thibault." She curtsied.

Thibault embraced her, a sickly experience, though Sabine kept the smile plastered on her face as she sat in the chair proffered by Thibault before she returned behind her large, ornate desk.

"And what brings you to me today?"

"I've come across some information that might be of interest to you."

"Interest?"

"Value, perhaps, is the better word."

Thibault's smile broadened. "I am always interested in valuable things. And just what is this valuable information?"

"What do you think it would be worth to the Templars to find out where one of their missing men is?"

Thibault's eyes narrowed slightly and she leaned back, her bearing different, as if she were no longer excited about learning something that could make her money. "Go on." Her voice was almost disinterested, with a hint of trepidation.

Is she scared of the Templars?

"There is a man being held in the prison for almost a month now. They're torturing him daily. I fear he doesn't have much longer to live."

"And what concern is that of mine?"

Sabine's eyes widened, slightly taken aback by the response.

The reward, of course!

"Well, I thought if the Templars knew, they might pay handsomely."

Thibault shook her head. "The prison serves the King, and he is no fan of the Templars. If a Templar is imprisoned there, I'm sure it's for good reason. The Templars have no reason to interfere with my business, but the King? He might have me arrested and tossed in with your prisoner."

Sabine's heart sank. Visions of purses filled with gold were evaporating as Thibault's words sank in. Interfering in the King's business was never wise. And if they found out she had been the one that told of his presence there, then she could lose her job, or worse.

Perhaps Thibault was right.

Perhaps she should keep her mouth shut.

Then something occurred to her, and her hope returned. "He didn't want to be freed."

Thibault's eyebrows rose. "Excuse me?"

"He didn't want to be freed. All he wanted was word to be sent to his master, so he might know that he hadn't broken his vow to him."

Thibault grunted. "If that's not a Templar's foolishness, I don't know what is." She sighed. "And what was this prisoner's name?"

Sabine shook her head. "I don't know, but he did give me the name of his master."

"And that was?"

"Sir Marcus de Rancourt."

A chair scraped nearby, in a room down the hall, and footfalls pounded toward them. Sabine's heart raced as she twisted in her chair to see who might be coming, then breathed a sigh of relief at the sight of a young man, slight in build though with a healthy countenance, standing in the door.

"Did you say 'Sir Marcus de Rancourt?'"

Sabine nodded. "I did." She eyed him. "Do you know him?"

But the young man ignored her, instead stepping deeper inside the room and addressing Thibault. "We have to help."

Thibault frowned, folding her arms. "And why would I want to do that?"

"It has to be his sergeant Simon, or one of his squires. These men helped you. They saved your life."

Thibault snorted. "And I repaid that favor by giving you a job, and forgiving three months' interest on a rather substantial loan. I owe them nothing."

"But, madam, please!"

She flicked her hand toward the door, dismissing them. "Get out. Both of you. This is the last I want to hear of this matter."

Enzo inhaled deeply, expanding his chest, his inflated frame even more intimidating, sending Sabine scrambling from the room while expressing her apologies for disturbing the woman. She hurried down the stairs, her nerves even more on edge as the young man followed her, the massive Enzo taking up the rear, though much more slowly.

She left the house and stepped onto the street, the young man joining her.

"Please, a word."

She looked about, watching for prying eyes, wishing this conversation was already over. "Quickly."

He pressed several coins into her hand, gaining her undivided attention. "Do what you can to help him. Extra food, water, whatever. And tell him a friend knows of his suffering, and that he will get word to his master. Tell him not to lose hope."

Sabine eyed the young man for a moment. "You know him?"

"I believe I do."

"And who should I say is his benefactor?"

"Thomas Durant."

La Conciergerie Prison
Paris, Kingdom of France

"Is anyone over there?"

Simon moaned, the pain from his latest torture session reasserting itself. His head pounded, his body throbbed, and his joints ached. And his parched mouth and sore throat from the screams and lack of drink, stifled any reply.

"I say, is anyone over there?"

Simon rolled over onto his stomach, struggling to push to his knees as he peered into the darkness surrounding him. "Who's there?" he asked, his voice raspy and weak.

"My name is Antoine. I'm in the cell next to you. Follow my voice, there's a hole in the wall."

A surge of excitement rushed through Simon at the prospect of actual human interaction. He forced himself forward, toward the voice that continued to urge him on, and when his own heavy breathing echoed back at him, he knew he had reached the wall.

"Don't be afraid. I'm a prisoner like you."

Simon ran his hand along the wall and found an opening. He reached through it, toward the voice, and his hand was suddenly grabbed. He clasped the other man's hand with what little strength he had left. The warmth of human contact overwhelmed him, and precious tears threatened to spill forth as he collapsed on the floor, spent, still gripping the hand.

"What's your name?"

102

"Simon."

The hand pumped his a few times. "Pleased to meet you, Simon."

Simon returned the shake, and noticed the man was missing a finger. He ran his thumb over the stump. "Did they do this to you?"

"Aye, they did, the bastards." The grip loosened and Simon let go of the man's hand, then repositioned so his face was in front of the hole. "I think they got a good laugh at that, they did."

"Why are you here?"

"They claim I robbed a lady, a member of the aristocracy. A lie, it is!"

Simon didn't care whether it was or not. All he cared about was that he was finally hearing a voice that wasn't filled with malice or evil. Beyond the woman whom he had spoken to, he had heard nothing friendly or civil.

He closed his eyes, a smile on his face. "Tell me about yourself, Antoine. Where are you from?"

"I was born in Chartres, but spend most of my time in Paris, selling my goods."

"What goods are those?"

"I make carvings. You know, from wood."

Simon pictured horses and other animals in proud poses, expertly carved, that young Pierre played with. "You must be good at it to make a living."

"Not much of one, but I keep my family fed, and that's all that really matters, isn't it?" He sighed. "Though now that they've taken my finger, I guess I'll have to figure out something new."

"Or adapt."

"I suppose I'll have to try, for the family's sake."

Simon nodded, though he couldn't truly empathize, not having a family of his own. He frowned, thinking of the women and children on the farm. Was he not responsible for them now? Yes, Marcus was ultimately responsible, but he had sworn an oath to protect them as well. Did that not make them his family, if not in the laws of man, then in the eyes of the Lord?

"Tell me of your family. Do you have any children?"

"Just the one at the moment. A son."

"What's his name?"

"Christian."

Simon gasped at the reply, picturing the boy he knew all those years ago, lying at the bottom of the well. "A-a fine name. And your wife?"

"Cateline. The most beautiful woman you could imagine."

Simon's eyes burned and his chest ached at Roland's wife's name. How could it be? How could there be a man, imprisoned in the cell next to him, with a wife named the same as the man he stood accused of murdering, and a son with the same name as the boy he was accused of murdering all those years ago.

A sharp pain seared through his head and he cried out, rolling onto his back as he gripped his skull.

"What's wrong?"

"My head! It hurts, it's as if it's going to explode!"

"Breathe, my friend. Try to empty your mind of any thoughts, then think of something that makes you happy and focus on that."

Simon desperately tried, but all he could think about was Christian falling, and imagining Roland's dead body—and to his horror, he was the one committing both atrocities. "I-I can't."

"Who is most important to you in your life?"

There wasn't a moment's hesitation. "Mar-Marcus!"

"Then picture him laughing."

Simon curled up in a ball, still squeezing his pounding head, his squinting eyes trying to picture his friend, and failing. He instead tried to imagine the red and white flag of the Templars, of the Order he had served for so long, and in the red fog of pain, he could almost see it.

Turn it into a tunic.

And it did. He focused on the tunic, then looked up and saw his master and friend, sitting in the saddle, his head tossed back, laughing at something said.

Then he smiled, the pounding fading, and as it did, he focused on the memory, his smile spreading as he pictured Jeremy, much younger than he was now, covered in horse manure after an ill-advised attempt to examine the bottom of his steed's hoof.

The horse was having none of it that day, and Jeremy didn't hear the end of it for years.

Good times.

The pounding was gone now, and he breathed easier as he tried to relax his muscles, lying flat on the hard floor.

"Are you all right?"

He nodded. "Yes, I think so."

"Good. I was worried about you. Something must have triggered a painful memory."

"Perhaps."

"You never did say why you're here."

Simon hesitated, then decided honesty was the best policy, not wanting to compound his troubles with the sin of lying with no possibility of confession. "I was falsely accused of murder."

"Oh, that is most unfortunate. This type here won't care if you're innocent or not. You'll hang for sure." There was a pause. "Did something I say remind you of your crimes? Perhaps that's what triggered your pain?"

Simon's eyes narrowed, wondering if that could be it. The names of his new friend's family had absolutely been mentioned only moments before his attack, though why he would react in such a manner was beyond him.

Because you feel guilty.

He frowned. He *did* feel guilty. He had already come to the conclusion that if he had never returned to his former home, Roland would still be alive. Christian's death was never his fault, and he felt no guilt there, but Roland was different. Though he hadn't committed the crime, he was in some way responsible.

His head throbbed again, and he quickly stifled the thoughts.

"Are you all right?"

Simon tried to focus. "Yes, just bad memories."

"Maybe if you told me about them, you'd feel better."

106

Simon sighed, leaning against the wall. "Perhaps."

The clang of the outer door to their cellblock opening had his stomach grumbling, and his hopes up as he wondered if it would be the same woman, and if she had news.

"Feeding time for you."

Simon paused, puzzled. "And not you?"

"They haven't fed me in days."

"Why not?"

"Remember that lady I supposedly robbed? I think she has a suitor with some pull around here. My guess is they've been instructed to let me die from starvation rather than face trial."

Simon frowned, then scurried toward the door as the small opening revealed a sliver of light. A plate was shoved through, then a cup of water. He moved them aside and pressed his face to the opening. "Psst!"

"Shhh!" admonished the woman. She shoved several bread rolls through the opening. "Don't let anyone see these."

He took them, his stomach audibly growling. "Thank you." He lowered his voice further. "Do you have any word on my master?"

"I was able to get word to someone who actually claims he knows you. He said to tell you that he will get word to your master, and to not lose hope."

Simon closed his eyes, relief sweeping over him. Though he had no doubt he would still die here, at least Marcus would know what had happened, and wouldn't go on thinking his friend and sergeant had abandoned his post. "What is his name?"

"I shouldn't say, in case they torture you and you reveal his identity before he succeeds."

Simon nodded, the woman clearly wise. "Agreed." He wanted to reach through the opening, to shake her hand, but didn't, the possibility of a guard within sight too great. "And thank you."

"You're welcome. Now I must go before they get suspicious."

"Very well." The opening snapped shut and Simon took his rations, much less meager than usual, back to the corner with the hole. "Give me your hand."

"Why?"

Simon chuckled. "Just stick your hand through."

"Give me a moment."

Simon could hear Antoine struggle on the other side then curse. "It won't fit."

Simon laughed. "It must be nice to not be skin and bone." He repositioned and shoved his hand with one of the rolls through the hole, his arm fitting with disappointing ease. "Take this."

He felt Antoine take the roll, then an excited gasp as he realized what it was. "Thank you, but...I can't accept this. I can't take food from a starving man."

"I have more. Trust me, eat it without guilt, my friend. Maybe, with some luck, we'll put some meat back on both our bones."

Simon couldn't understand the reply, Antoine's mouth obviously full. Simon made quick work of his meal and water, and with the renewed sense of hope he felt with the news a friend had been contacted, he gripped the final roll in his hand, deciding there was another in greater need.

He shoved his hand through the hole. "Here, take this."

"No, you've already been too generous."

"Please."

There was a heavy sigh. "Very well, who am I to refuse food from a fool?" Simon smiled as Antoine took the second roll. "Thank you, my friend, you truly are the answer to my prayers."

Simon leaned back in the corner and closed his eyes, content for the first time in over a month. He gave the Lord thanks for the food, for the company of a good man, and the bravery of a young woman.

And prayed his master would soon know his fate.

Le Chesnay, Kingdom of France

It was a waste of time. Nobody was talking. He had been stonewalled by silence, glares, and outright hostility at every turn, and was no closer to discovering anything beyond what he already knew. He was positive the body in the fire wasn't Simon's, yet to truly prove it to others, he needed to know whose body it actually was.

And nobody was willing to help.

He spotted the old lady who, when he had arrived, directed him to Simon's home. He walked over to her with as pleasant a smile as he could muster. "Might I trouble you once again?"

She frowned, regarding him for a moment. "It might be the death of me, but ask your question."

He decided not to waste it on asking why it might put her at risk, for he feared she had chosen her words carefully, and he might indeed be limited to a single question. "I'm looking for a man with a crooked back, who would have gone missing about a month ago."

Her eyes widened slightly, the question clearly not what she was expecting. She shrugged. "Doesn't sound like anyone from around here."

"Then a traveler perhaps?"

"Most likely. I'm sure I'd know if one of the townsfolk were missing."

Marcus smiled slightly, her observation astute. "Any idea who might know?"

She shrugged again. "I'd try the inns and taverns,

but you'll have no luck here."

Marcus eyed her. "Why?"

"No one will talk to you. They know why you're asking."

"Yet you do."

"I'm an old woman with no family left. What can they do to me?"

"Who?"

She warily eyed a man nearby whom Marcus had noticed earlier, paying a little too much attention to their conversation. Marcus stared at him and the man turned, walking across the street, toward the Bailiff's Delegate's office.

That's not good.

"Is there anyone who might answer my questions?"

She lowered her voice, leaning in closer, and jerked her head down the road. "Just out of town there's an inn. Ask for Mrs. Dubois. She might be willing to talk. She takes in all manner of people, including the cripples the folks around here won't touch lest they catch something."

Marcus smiled slightly. "I thank you, my good lady." He mounted his horse, then nodded to her. "I'm sorry you couldn't help me."

She gave him a grateful look, her face becoming stern. "As I said, I've got nothing to say to you. Now be off, and don't disturb me again!"

Marcus turned in his saddle and headed for the outskirts of the town, anger on his face to make the others hopefully think he wasn't pleased with his conversation. He feared for the old woman, though he

111

had a feeling she didn't share it. She, like the others, seemed to be just living their days, awaiting death.

Something more was going on, and he desperately wanted to know what it was.

I wonder if Simon figured it out.

If that were the case, then it might explain things. Could this Roland person have been involved, and Simon was forced to kill him? He doubted that. He would have said something. What was more likely, was that Simon had stumbled upon something, and whoever was behind it, framed him so he would be arrested and executed.

Yet he still felt that wasn't at all what was going on, at least with Simon. He had no doubt something untoward was happening here. People were simply too scared, and it most likely involved Gilles Laurent and his men. But with respect to Simon, that was likely related to what had happened thirty years ago, and how the truth might disrupt Gilles' position, and whatever schemes he might be up to.

Yet none of that was his concern. Simon might be alive, out there, somewhere, and he had to find him. And to do that, he needed leverage over Gilles, and at the moment, the only leverage he could think of was the truth.

He spotted the inn and rode up the tree-lined path to the door. He tied up his horse and pointed at the ground, ordering Tanya to stay. She sat, her tail wagging as she stared up at him, her tongue hanging out. He gave her a scratch behind an ear then stepped inside, the ground floor filled with tables and chairs, and few customers.

A woman stood in the far corner, tending a large

cauldron over a healthy fire, and he made the probably safe assumption that this was Mrs. Dubois, and perhaps his only hope at answers.

He approached her and she turned, her eyes widening with surprise at the sight of his surcoat. "A Templar Knight, in my establishment! I would say my prospects must be rising if I didn't know better."

He smiled. "I'm not sure I understand."

"I need paying customers, not those sworn to poverty."

Marcus chuckled. "Madam, I am Sir Marcus de Rancourt. Might you be Mrs. Dubois?"

"And how might you know that?"

"Someone in town said you might be able to help me with a rather delicate matter."

She glanced about the room then pointed to a nearby table. They sat on opposite sides, and she flicked her wrist at him. "Out with it, Templar. I haven't got all day."

He smiled. "I'm wondering if you might have seen a man come through, about a month ago, with a bent back. He likely would have leaned to his left quite dramatically."

She nodded. "Yes, I saw him. Tried to rob me, he did. The little bastard was no match for my stick, though!" She pointed toward a substantial piece of wood on a nearby table. "I gave him a good thrashing, then Laurent's men arrested him and took him away. Haven't seen him since." She eyed him. "Why?"

Marcus smiled. "Just trying to get something straight, that's all."

She grunted. "Aren't we all." She sighed. "Can I feed you, at least. God knows I won't have enough customers today to finish what I've cooked."

Marcus glanced around. "Business isn't good?"

"There have been problems on the road."

Marcus recalled his encounter. "Highwaymen?"

She shrugged. "That's what some say."

"I encountered some on the road in."

She eyed him, then laughed. "Only fools would rob a Templar. Four *deniers*! What good is that, that it's worth dying for?"

Marcus smiled. "They apparently agreed with you."

Somebody at a nearby table growled. "You talk too much, Madame."

She glared at the eavesdropper. "This is my establishment, and I'll say what I want, to whom I want. Now drink in silence, Mathis, or leave!"

The man downed his drink then rose, slamming the cup down on the table. He jabbed a finger at her. "You be watching yourself. A loose tongue is liable to find itself removed."

Marcus began to rise when the man waved him off. "Keep your seat, Templar, I'm leaving." The man shuffled through the door, his legs unsteady, drink clearly his master.

Marcus turned to Dubois. "What was that about?"

"He's a local. A drunkard. Most won't serve him anymore as he tends to let his fists fly when he's had too much, but, well, I need the business." She sighed. "He is right about one thing, however. I *have* said too much. My husband would probably tan my hide if he knew what I've said, but I'm tired of being afraid in my own home." She stared out the window. "I grew up here, and it isn't right."

Marcus leaned closer, lowering his voice. "Who are you afraid of?"

The few customers that remained all leaned closer in their chairs, the creaks visibly sending shivers through Dubois' body. "Like I said, I've wagged my tongue too long already." She leaned closer, her voice barely a whisper. "I will say this. You must be careful. These parts aren't safe for anyone who asks questions."

Crécy-la-Chapelle, Kingdom of France

Thomas Durant rode into the village of Crécy-la-Chapelle, drinking in the small-town desolation surrounding him. It was winter, so nothing seemed alive except for the people, and even they seemed barely so. Perhaps it was the lack of them. Paris was always bustling. Even at night, the streets held more people than these streets at midday.

Or perhaps he should say 'street,' for there was only one.

Sir Marcus had offered him a home here, a job on the farm and a roof over his head, and he had turned it down, not wanting to abandon the home of his late father, the only home he had ever known.

Then barely weeks later, Sir Marcus and his men had discovered him near death, starving, in that very home. He had been prepared to join them in their humble surroundings, but circumstances intervened.

Simone Thibault, to be exact.

She was a horrible woman, and he hated working for her.

But the money was beyond anything he could have ever imagined.

He was paid at the end of every week more than his father at the best of times could have earned in a month. And all that was asked of him was to read and write, and do some accounting work with her books. His father's line of work, that of a forger, had prepared him well, his father insisting he learn to read and write and do basic math, with the eventual

116

expectation, Thomas was sure, that he take over the family business.

Alas, he had absolutely no skills when it came to drawing, unfortunately ruling out the forging of documents.

His particular talents were nearly worthless in the slums of Paris, but to a woman like Thibault, they were invaluable.

And that was unfortunate.

If she paid him a pauper's wage, he might be tempted to give it up and move to a place such as this, but with the wages so good, he was eating better than he ever had, the fire was always stoked, providing him the warmest winter he had ever experienced, and he was actually taking some pride in himself for the first time since he could remember.

Yet there was a pit in his stomach that hollowed out a little more each day, ever-increasingly causing him distress as he thought of what the numbers he dealt with represented.

Debts owed by people as desperate as he once was.

He hadn't met these people, though had heard their voices through the walls as they pleaded for leniency from the heartless woman that now employed him.

And it was his numbers over which they were begging forgiveness.

Yet he hadn't loaned them the money. He hadn't forced them to borrow it. He hadn't created the circumstances that had driven these people into the hands of Thibault.

These were the excuses he used to make himself feel better at night as he lay in his bed, a cup of wine in hand, and more food on his lap for a snack than he used to eat in an entire day when his father was still alive to provide for him.

It was these luxuries, these indulgences, that made it so easy to overlook whom he worked for, and he kept telling himself that all he was doing was tallying numbers. He never saw whom those numbers represented. He never interacted with them. God would forgive him.

Wouldn't he?

He wasn't so sure of that.

He asked for directions to the farm, and a friendly man pointed the way. He was soon riding up the path leading to a humble, and by all outward appearances, recently expanded home. Though humble wouldn't be an entirely accurate description for these parts, the glass in the windows a luxury most around here didn't appear to be able to afford, and a luxury even he hadn't considered until now.

How his neighbors would be jealous if they saw actual glass in his windows.

And how quickly the local children would break such windows.

He heard a shout from a barn atop a gently sloping hill, someone waving to him, another following as they both jogged toward him. Children, bundled up against the cold, raced from behind the house, giggling, and coming to a rapid halt in front of him, their eyes wide with excitement at a visitor.

Thomas dismounted and nodded at the children, unsure of what to say. "Umm, good day."

The biggest stepped forward. "I'm Jacques de Foix. Who are you?"

"Thomas!" cried David as he neared. "What brings you here? Have you come to your senses and decided to join us?"

Thomas smiled at the two squires he had come to know a couple of months ago. He shook his head. "No, I'm afraid I've come with possibly troubling news."

"Thomas!"

He turned toward the house to see Lady Joanne standing in the doorway with a beaming smile. He bowed. "Lady Joanne."

She beckoned him over, shaking her head. "Please, no such formalities are needed here, I assure you. Come in from the cold, you must be frozen to the bone. Have you come directly from Paris?"

He nodded, stepping inside the home, the warmth from the fire welcoming. "Yes. I've been traveling all morning. I would have come yesterday, but I wasn't able to extricate myself from my responsibilities before it was too late to travel safely. I only hope it isn't too late."

Joanne indicated for Thomas to sit, and her chambermaid, Beatrice, handed him a steaming cup of something. He took a sip and smiled at the tisane.

"Thank you."

David sat beside him, Jeremy leaning against the now closed door. "What is your troubling news?"

"A woman you may remember, Sabine, came to Mrs. Thibault's office yesterday."

David's eyes narrowed. "Why do I know that name?"

Joanne raised a finger. "Isn't she the one whom Mrs. Thibault had fake an illness, so she could put her

119

girl inside the prison in her place?"

Thomas smiled. "You have an excellent memory, Milady."

Jeremy grunted. "Not to be rude, but please, what news could you have that is so troubling? Is it about Simon? We haven't heard from him in over a month."

The room became serious, and even more so as Thomas nodded. "I wasn't sure who it might be until I arrived and saw you two were safe. Sabine told Mrs. Thibault that someone in La Conciergerie Prison, who was being tortured daily and was near death, begged her to get word to Sir Marcus. She didn't know who it was, but I knew it must be one of you two, or Simon. If he has been missing, then I fear it must be him that is being held."

David cursed, then immediately apologized to the ladies in the room. "But this makes no sense. Did she say why he was imprisoned?"

Thomas shook his head. "I fear she knew precious little. I gave her some money, told her to help him as best she could, and to tell him that I would get word to Sir Marcus." He looked about, realizing for the first time that Marcus hadn't yet made his presence known. "Where is he?"

David frowned. "He went looking for Simon. We're hoping to hear from him shortly, but I fear there's no time to waste. If Simon is in custody, I am certain it isn't a righteous imprisonment, which means Sir Marcus probably has no idea he is there. We must get word to him at once."

Jeremy stood straight. "I'll go have a message sent."

David held up a hand, stopping him. "No. If

Simon has been imprisoned, then something more is going on, and Sir Marcus has no idea what he is getting himself into. He might need help."

Jeremy bit a knuckle. "But our orders?" He gestured at the women, then the children hiding behind the door in the next room as they listened in on what the adults were discussing. "We're not to leave them."

Joanne settled it. "This new information has changed things. Sir Marcus must be warned, and Simon must be saved. It is your duty to go to them. We will be all right on our own."

David chewed his cheek for a moment, then turned to Thomas. "Can you stay with them?"

Thomas tensed, his mouth opening slightly. "Umm, well, Mrs. Thibault is expecting me back tomorrow, so, umm…"

"Please, Master Thomas, you must stay. I won't rest easy if I leave these helpless—"

"Helpless!" exploded Joanne, leaving David to blush.

"Umm, perhaps I chose my words poorly."

"I should say you did!" Joanne leaned forward, patting Thomas on the hand. "Stay here with us, and we'll send word to Mrs. Thibault that I insisted, as there was an urgent matter that required your assistance. If that doesn't satisfy her, I'll travel there myself with you to straighten things out. All right?"

Thomas wasn't sure what to do. He doubted any amount of convincing from Lady Joanne would be enough to satisfy Thibault, though when this business was over with, Sir Marcus might succeed where she failed.

And it's the right thing to do.

He decided it might be good for his soul, and could, perhaps, put him back in the Lord's good graces. He nodded, forcing a smile. "I shall be honored to stay, though I dare say I may be the one who needs the assistance of these fine ladies should any danger come to pass."

Joanne beamed at him, a graceful hand held out toward him as she eyed David. "Now *that's* how you talk to a lady."

David blushed. "I shall endeavor to do better in the future, Milady."

Joanne laughed, along with Beatrice. "Now, is there time for you to depart tonight, or should you wait until morning?"

David stared out the window. "I believe we can reach Paris tonight. We'll stay at the headquarters there, and send a message to Mrs. Thibault on your behalf, Master Thomas, and a message to Sir Marcus at the Versailles Commandry."

Joanne stood, everyone else immediately joining her. "Very well. You two ready the horses, and we will prepare you some provisions for your journey. Three days?"

David shook his head. "Just for the day is all. We'll resupply in Paris."

Joanne grunted. "We'll give you three days' worth. You won't be eating that slop when you can have good, home-cooked food."

Thomas smiled at the exchange as David acquiesced, then left with Jeremy to prepare the horses. This was a home, despite there being no blood relations under the roof beyond the two children born here.

It was a place in which he might, perhaps, be happy.

It was a place that might save his soul.

La Conciergerie Prison
Paris, Kingdom of France

Simon savored the last bite of the extra roll the young woman, whose name he did not know, and feared to ask, had provided him yet again. He smiled at the moans of pleasure coming from the other side of the stone wall separating him from his companion, Antoine.

"I do believe that was the best-tasting thing I have ever eaten."

Simon had to agree. "It was something, wasn't it?"

"If I ever get out of here, I think I shall eat nothing but rolls for the rest of my life."

Simon chuckled. "I fear my fate is to die here, but perhaps your fate is to return to your family. I pray every chance I get that this comes to pass."

Antoine sighed. "You are a good man, Simon Chastain. A better man than I."

Simon lay down flat on the floor, his ear positioned near the hole joining the two cells, a hole that had saved him, he was certain, from insanity. "I wouldn't say that, my friend. You won the heart of a wonderful woman, the Lord blessed you with a healthy boy, and the gift of a skill in demand to provide for your family. It sounds to me that in the eyes of the Lord, you are the better man."

Antoine chuckled. "Then why am I here, my friend?"

"Evil exists in this world. I've witnessed it far too

often to be able to deny it exists. But I've also seen that good triumphs over evil eventually. Sometimes it takes longer than us mere mortals think it should, but in the end, good shall be victorious."

"I pray this is true, my brother, and it may be for me, as the crimes I'm accused of are minor compared to yours, but how, pray tell, can good possibly triumph over the evil that challenges you?"

Simon closed his eyes, clasping his hands across his chest. "I will die here, in this prison, but justice will prevail. Once my master knows what has happened to me, and why, he will clear my good name, bring those responsible to justice, and my soul shall rest in peace."

"But you'll still be dead."

Simon smiled. "I've never feared death. I've lived a good, long life, in service to my brothers and the Lord. I've seen wonders that most men can't even imagine, and comradery few can understand. If I die here, in this prison, accused of a crime I never committed, then so be it. The Lord must feel it is necessary. Perhaps my death will bring those responsible to justice, and that is the purpose I am meant to serve."

"If it were me, I'd be asking the Lord to figure out a way that lets me live."

Simon chuckled. "You make me laugh, my friend. I don't mean to sound selfish, as I would wish for your sake that you weren't here, sharing this hell with me, but I am grateful that the good Lord put us together. It has certainly made these past days much more pleasant."

"And mine, as well." He heard shuffling, and then Antoine's voice became louder, as if he were speaking directly into the hole. "Perhaps we should try to figure a way out for you."

Simon turned his head toward the hole. "I'm not sure what you mean. Escape?"

"No, nothing so grandiose. There's no escaping from here. What I mean is, perhaps you should tell them what they want to hear."

"But they haven't asked me anything."

"Nothing?"

"Not a single thing has been asked of me."

"Perhaps that is because they feel you already know the question."

Simon thought for a moment. It was an interesting notion. Why ask an obvious question? The immediate answer was also obvious—to get the answer quicker. But that would end the torture, and it was quite evident that those responsible for his suffering were taking great pleasure in inflicting pain, and an answer might end their fun.

"But what *is* the question?"

"You don't know?"

Simon grunted. "Evidently."

"Confessing to your crimes, of course."

Simon frowned. "But I'm not guilty."

"Does it matter?"

"Of course it matters!"

"To men like us, yes, but does it matter to our Lord? He knows the truth. A false confession here means nothing in the afterlife. Confess to these crimes you have been accused of, and all your suffering could be over, and perhaps you might even see the light of day, should mercy be granted."

Simon frowned, staring up at the darkness overhead as he considered Antoine's words. The man was right. The confession would mean nothing in the eyes of the Lord. But there was one thing Antoine was forgetting, one thing he couldn't possibly understand.

He was a Templar.

And Templars didn't confess to crimes they didn't commit.

Even if it meant their death.

Le Chesnay, Kingdom of France

"You're sure this happened? You haven't exactly been a reliable source in the past."

Mathis' head bobbed rapidly. "Absolutely. I'd only had two drinks, I swear."

"And this Templar came in, asking questions about a man with a crooked back?"

"Yes. And Mrs. Dubois was quite liberal with her answers."

The man sitting across from him frowned, clearly displeased, and that was rarely good for those around him, if past experience was any indication. "She's always been a problem."

Mathis agreed emphatically, now wondering if coming here was such a good idea. He could have ignored what he had heard, but his intoxicated tongue was an undisciplined one. Yet he also had a choice after he stormed out of Dubois' establishment. He could have just gone home, but no, his idiotic mind had the notion that informing on her might lead to some coin, and that might lead to more drink.

He regretted what he was about to say before the words even came out of his mouth, but his inebriated brain was too slow to stop his tongue. "She certainly seemed to be willing to talk of your business, that's for sure."

Pursed lips and piercing eyes were the reply.

And silence.

A bead of sweat ran down Mathis' spine, quickly

followed by another, as perspiration dampened his upper lip and forehead. He began to shake, from either fear or lack of drink—which, he wasn't sure.

Several coins were produced. "Let me know anything else you hear about this Templar."

Mathis grabbed the coins and bowed his way out of the office. "Of course, sir, of course."

He stepped out into the cold and the door was slammed shut behind him.

"He's trouble."

Mathis froze, cocking an ear.

"Do you want me to take care of him?" asked one of the others that had stood in silence the entire time.

"Not now."

Mathis breathed a sigh of relief.

"But when this is all over, perhaps."

The sigh had been wasted.

"It's this Templar I'm more concerned with. I thought with Simon out of the way, we might be able to get back to normal around here, but with this knight now asking questions, I think he may be trouble. He's figured out that the man in the fire wasn't his sergeant, that much is obvious. If he keeps digging, he just might cause us some inconveniences I'm not willing to have."

"You want him dead?"

"Yes. But do it quietly, out of town. I don't want any witnesses." A chair scraped on the floor. "And I don't want anybody finding the body. Ever."

"Yes, sir."

"Oh, and take care of Mrs. Dubois. She's been a thorn in my side for too long."

"I'll take care of it right away."

Footsteps approached the door and Mathis rushed down the street, his heart hammering, the coins in his hand feeling like thirty pieces of silver.

And drink for a week.

La Conciergerie Prison
Paris, Kingdom of France

"My friend, sometimes I wonder if you enjoy the pain."

Simon's eyebrows rose at Antoine's observation. "What makes you say that?"

"You didn't confess, did you."

Simon grunted. "No."

"Why not?"

"You wouldn't understand."

"What, that you're a Templar, and Templars don't confess to crimes they didn't commit?"

Simon's closed eyes shot open as he rolled onto his side, his mouth mere inches from the hole. "Are you some sort of sorcerer?"

"Excuse me?"

"I was thinking that very thing before."

"I have many gifts, or so you tell me, but none are the ability to read the minds of men. It would come in handy, though. Perhaps then I wouldn't have stolen that woman's money."

Simon pursed his lips, his body tensing slightly. "So they were right. You *are* a thief."

"I'm sorry I lied to you, Simon, I truly am. But a man never admits guilt in prison, certainly not to strangers. But you, I now think of as my friend, and I cannot lie to my friend."

Simon sighed. The man was right. Lies within these walls were inevitable, at least with the common man. And no one deserved this sort of punishment, not for the theft of a purse. "Why did you do it?"

"You won't like the answer."

Simon returned to lying on his back, a smile on his face. "Try me."

"She insulted my craftsmanship."

Simon's eyebrows rose. "And you robbed her for that?"

"Not my finest hour, I assure you. I'd never done anything like that before in my entire life, but she did it so loudly, that all within earshot could hear her. These were my customers she was scaring away, and only because my offerings weren't up to her standards. What kind of an idiot thinks that those who shop the markets I frequent could afford the prices I'd have to charge in order to sell the quality she expects?

"Does she have any idea how many hours of extra work would go into polishing a carving to a sheen? To stain them certain colors? My wares are for the poor with a little bit of extra money to buy a loved one a trinket on a special occasion. Most of my business is done around Christmas, when parents are looking to acquire a toy for their child. And this fool insults me because my work isn't of the quality someone like her could afford. She's lucky I only took her purse!"

Simon chuckled. "I understand your frustration, my friend, though it is still no excuse for breaking one of the Commandments."

"I know, I know, though don't you think I've been punished enough?"

"I do. And I have a suggestion for you."

"What is that?"

"Tell the guards that you are ready to apologize to

the woman, in person, and explain to them what you just told me. In kinder words, of course."

"Are you trying to get rid of me, or get me killed?"

Simon laughed. "If it gets you killed, then you were going to die anyway. But if, in the calm that time has bought over these past days, she might be made to understand—from a humble and apologetic man— how her words hurt you, perhaps the charges might be dropped. Perhaps you could offer to create a piece of work that she would consider worthy of her home, for no charge."

"Ahh, you're trying to force me into the hands of the loan sharks like that wench Thibault!"

Simon's heart beat a little faster. "*Simone* Thibault?"

"Why, yes. I'm surprised a Templar would have reason to know of her."

Simon frowned. "I had occasion to encounter her a couple of months ago on another matter with my master. It is odd, that, you knowing her too. I know only one person of such reputation in all the city, and it happens to be the same one you know."

There was a chuckle. "I'm sorry to correct you, my friend, but I know many of her type, though she is the only *woman* I know who is in the business."

Simon grunted. "She is definitely unusual, that one." He rolled back toward the hole. "But back to what I was saying. I think you should confess."

"Instead of yourself?"

Simon smiled. "You know what I mean. You just might find yourself out of here before you know it."

"You'd be lost without me."

"I'd survive."

"Are you sure? It took me three days to get you to even acknowledge that I was here."

Simon's heart skipped a beat. "What do you mean?"

"I was calling to you for three days before you answered me."

Simon shook his head as he recalled their initial conversation. "That's impossible. I heard you as plain as day."

"Perhaps on the day you finally replied and gave me bread. But before that, you were only mumbling in pain, something about asking someone for forgiveness. I couldn't really make much out."

Simon rolled to a sitting position, his legs crossed, as he recalled their first conversation. He did have to admit the beginning was foggy. He had just returned from being tortured, so that might have something to do with it. And being tortured every day, perhaps that was why he hadn't heard Antoine at first. His body was screaming in pain, his senses overwhelmed, his mind plagued by torturous headaches that created a searing, piercing noise in his head.

It began to return, and he took a deep, slow breath, as he tried to calm down.

"I'm sorry, Antoine, but I don't remember that."

"Nor should I expect you to, after what they've put you through."

Simon sighed, returning to his prone position. "Perhaps I *would* be lost without you, though my suffering should be no reason to risk your freedom. The next time they take you, do as I say, and ask to speak to your accuser. Then I hope to never see you again."

134

"Be careful what you wish for, Simon Chastain. I might just follow your advice."

Simon smiled, then his heart slammed at the outer cell door opening. He struggled to his feet, backing into the corner, preparing for whatever was to come, but his door never opened.

It was Antoine's that did.

"Your time has come, convict!"

"No, please, I didn't mean to steal from her. I was angry. I'm sorry."

Sounds of a struggle broke Simon's heart as he slid down the wall and onto the floor, his friend begging for mercy, the sounds of a vicious beating being delivered before it finally stopped, only the groans of a broken man now heard, then sounds of a body dragged along the floor and out into the corridor, the heavy cell door slamming shut.

He wanted to call out to him, to give him encouragement, but he dared not. If the guards knew they had been communicating, it could make things far worse for both of them.

Instead, he crawled to his knees and clasped his hands in front of him, staring up toward the heavens as tears streamed down his cheeks. And shame pulsed throughout him as he realized the tears were not just for what had become of his friend, but also for the fact he was now alone, perhaps never to hear a friendly voice again.

He opened his eyes, picturing the face of his Lord, and begged forgiveness for his selfish thoughts.

"Please, Lord, if someone must be punished, punish me, not him. He has a family to take care of, and I have no one. If someone must be sacrificed, let it be me."

He bowed his head, listening for a response he knew would never come.

And sighed, collapsing to his side and curling into a ball of physical and mental anguish. He pictured Marcus, and rather than an image of him on the battlefield, or somewhere in the Holy Land, he saw him milking a cow.

He smiled.

Of all the memories!

His mind was flooded with images of the farm, of the children, and even the women.

And each image broadened his smile.

The farm was his home.

It was where he belonged.

And he never should have doubted that.

Le Chesnay, Kingdom of France

Marcus stared at the boots laid out on the table, all finely crafted, suitable for any traveler that might be coming through. He nodded at the man whose hand was behind the work.

"You are truly skilled."

"Thank you. Are you interested in a pair?"

Marcus chuckled. "The Order provides all I need." He tapped the toe of one of the boots. "I'm afraid I could never afford anything as fine as this."

"That's unfortunate. Then you'll be moving along, won't you."

Marcus regarded the man. He sensed no maliciousness in the rudeness, just fear. This man clearly didn't want to be seen speaking with a Templar.

Marcus smiled pleasantly. "Of course. But first, if I may. Did you see or hear anything the night of the fire?"

The man's eyes widened slightly, followed by an emphatic headshake. "No."

"Very well. A good day to you." Marcus continued his casual stroll, Tanya at his side, examining the offerings, exchanging pleasantries with the travelers who had no reason to fear him, and continued to admire certain items, and ask his question.

And continued to be sent away empty-handed.

On his umpteenth rejection, he spotted a man behind the stalls, between two buildings, staring at him. The man jerked his head, as if beckoning him, then disappeared between the buildings. Marcus didn't acknowledge him, instead continuing his stroll, then after a moment or two, stepped through a gap in the vendors and between two buildings. He walked with purpose between them, coming out the back, then turned to his left to find the man standing about twenty paces away, staring toward the market.

Marcus cleared his throat and the poor man almost fainted in shock. He quickly recovered.

"I hear you've been asking questions."

Marcus nodded. "I have. Do you have answers?"

"I might, if the price were right."

Marcus smiled. "I'm a Templar, sworn to poverty. I'm afraid I have nothing to offer but my thanks."

The man frowned. "A lot of good that will do. Does thanks put food on my table?"

"No, but it might put you in good with the Lord, and *He* might put food on your table."

The man considered him for a moment, then sighed. "Well, I've stuck my neck out already, haven't I? You want to know about the fire."

"I do."

"Well, you didn't hear this from me, but I was out that night, getting some firewood, when I saw a cart pull up. There was a fight, then the fire broke out and that friend of yours was killed."

"Then what happened?"

"Nothing much. They rounded up some prisoners that had escaped, loaded them in the back of the cart, and left."

Marcus tried not to get excited. "And these

prisoners, you're certain none of them were my sergeant?"

The man shrugged. "Everyone knows Simon is the body that continues to be defiled to this day in the ruins."

Marcus stepped closer, lowering his voice. "And what if I told you that it wasn't Simon at all that lay there?"

"I'd say what proof do you have?"

"The man who died had a bent spine. He could never swing a sword, and would have walked hunched over. When you saw Simon upon his return, did he at all appear like this?"

The man's eyes widened. "He sat as tall in his saddle as I had ever seen. A fine figure of a man, he was." The man smiled. "Then that might explain something I heard said that night."

Marcus restrained himself. "What did you hear?"

"I heard a man yell something about how his master would have revenge upon them all."

"Was this before or after the fire?"

"Toward the end, I should think. I heard the man who burned die a most horrible death, then those words were spoken by one of the survivors. Could you be the master he spoke of?"

Marcus frowned. "I fear so." He pursed his lips. "And you have no idea where this cart went?"

The man shook his head.

"In what direction did it leave?"

The man pointed. "Toward Paris, though there are many places they could have gone between here and there."

139

Marcus agreed. "Have the other prisoners been seen since?"

The man shook his head. "Once you get arrested in this town, you're seldom seen again. That's why nobody risks doing anything to draw attention to themselves."

"Yet here you are."

The man grunted. "I'm a fool who believes in justice, I suppose. I never did believe the stories they told of Simon when we were kids. He wasn't the type to lose his temper. There's no way he killed Christian, of that I'm sure."

Marcus regarded the man. He was about the right age to have been around in those years. "Do many feel that way?"

"Unfortunately, no, or if they do, they're too terrified to say anything."

"Why?"

The man shook his head. "I've said enough already. I've told you what you wanted to know about the fire, and I dare say you liked what you heard, if your expression is any indication. But I do have to live here, I do have a business to run. If anyone saw us talking, word could get to the wrong people, and I'd be in big trouble, I tell you. I'd probably be buried in the same hole those others are buried in, where your sergeant probably is."

Marcus frowned. "Let's hope that isn't true."

"Oh, it's true all right. Your Simon crossed the wrong people, and they have too much to protect. I suggest you leave now, while you still can. There's nothing for you here, only death."

Marcus smiled. "I've encountered Death on many

occasions, and bested him every time." He wiped the smile off his face. "And I still believe Simon is alive, and I won't rest until I either find him, or his body."

"I fear it is *your* body they will find."

His stomach grumbled and Tanya whimpered in response. He patted it. "Perhaps, but not at this moment, for I am hungry, and the good Lord would never let me die on an empty stomach."

Dubois' Inn
Le Chesnay, Kingdom of France

Mrs. Dubois swept the thresh beyond the hold and out the door, the old straw having served its purpose for too long. Her husband would be back before long with a fresh batch, and it would be spread about to once again keep the floor serviceable for her guests.

She looked about.

What guests?

Business kept getting worse, and the only way it would get better would be to give in, yet she refused. Her husband wanted to, but she had threatened to cut him off if he dared.

He had acquiesced, a roll in the hay more important to him than winning an argument.

Though soon they might not have any choice. With word being spread not to frequent their establishment, soon they wouldn't be able to afford to live off the scraps of those who had no choice but to come here.

She sighed, then cursed the Lord for allowing this to happen to them.

Then immediately apologized.

He understands.

The door swung open behind her as she wiped down a table. "We're not serving for another hour, but you're welcome to wait by the fire and warm yourself."

There was no reply.

She straightened, turning toward the door to find it closed, a man standing in the shadows. "Are you deaf or mute?"

The sound of a sword drawing from a sheath had her heart racing.

She screamed.

But there was no one to hear it, beyond her assailant.

She rushed toward the back and the only other entrance. The sounds of chairs and tables being knocked out of the way as the man pursued her, only caused her to run that much faster, and she cursed for letting herself get so fat.

She pushed through to the back room, the door in sight. She grabbed the handle and threw the door open, glancing over her shoulder as she squeezed through, the frigid cold immediately making its presence felt.

There was no rage in the man's eyes, just determination.

And she recognized him.

And she knew she should have given in.

She went to the left, along the back of their inn, continuing to scream for help, then rounded the corner. She pushed forward as quickly as she could, and looked back when she heard a grunt then curse, smiling only briefly at the sight of the man having fallen as he made the corner.

She was in the open now, but with the isolated location, there would be no one to help her, and nowhere to hide.

She was going to die.

She prayed for forgiveness of all her sins as the heavy footfalls drew closer, then closed her eyes as he was almost upon her.

So she didn't see the beast, instead only hearing its angry snarl as it bounded toward her. She opened her eyes and screamed anew as a massive black dog leaped through the air at her. She dropped to her knees and it thankfully flew over her, missing her by mere inches.

But she wasn't the target.

She turned to see the beast clamp its mighty jaws on the forearm of the man, the sword clattering to the ground as he screamed in terror, shaking back and forth as he tried to rid himself of the mastiff now gripping him.

This is your chance!

She pushed to her feet and continued to run toward the road, when she saw the Templar Knight from earlier galloping toward her.

And cried in relief.

He leaped from his horse, rushing toward her as he drew his sword. "Are you all right, Mrs. Dubois?"

She nodded, gasping for air and clasping her chest. "I am now, thanks to your beast."

He raced past her. "Tanya, break!"

She let go immediately, clearly a well-trained dog, sitting on her haunches, panting happily. Marcus scratched her behind the ears, then pressed his sword against the now prone man's chest.

"Who are you?"

"I'm nobody! Just a traveler!"

Liar!

But she bit her tongue. If she revealed the truth, it

144

could mean more trouble for her, and it would absolutely lead to more questions from the Templar, questions she'd feel obligated to answer since he had saved her life.

Yet she had to save her own. This Templar would be gone soon, yet she'd remain behind, struggling to survive with the likes of the ilk now lying on her property.

"Then why were you accosting this woman!"

The bastard stole a quick glance at her, and she made a point of returning his stare. With a clamped jaw.

"I-I wasn't! She started screaming when I drew my sword to place it on the table. I was running after her to tell her it was all right, then I got scared, and thought she might make trouble for me with her ruckus."

Marcus turned to her. "Do you believe him?"

She could tell he didn't. Not for a moment. She shrugged, then stared at the ground. "I suppose it isn't, umm, outside the realm of possibility. I have been known to overreact on occasion."

Marcus frowned, clearly not believing her, but deciding she had her reasons for what she said. He stepped back, removing his sword from the man's chest. "Be off with you! And if I ever see you near this woman again, I'll take your head."

The man's eyes bulged and he struggled to his feet, rushing toward a nearby horse, nursing his shredded arm. He mounted with difficulty, then raced away, not saying a word, Marcus glaring at him, the dog growling her goodbye.

Marcus turned toward her. "Now, why don't you

tell me what's really going on?"

She stared at her feet. Or she would have if she could see them. "I'm sure I don't know what you mean."

"You knew who that man was, and he had every intention of killing you. Why?"

She sighed, then stared up at him. "You saved my life, and you deserve answers for it, but I can't give them to you. All you've done is buy me another day of life, unless I rectify what brought this on, which I intend to do in short order."

Marcus pursed his lips, regarding her for a moment. "I think you are mistaken as to what this is about."

Her eyes widened slightly. "What do you mean?"

Marcus waved an arm toward the town in the distance. "I don't know what is going on here, but something definitely is. Everyone is afraid to talk, and I suspect I know why. I won't press you for more information, madam, as I can see in your eyes that the very notion terrifies you. But I will say this. The man who just tried to kill you, most likely was doing so because you were seen talking to me. Whatever reason you think this is about, and the remedy you think will resolve it, won't. This has nothing to do with that, and I fear these people will not stop until you are dead."

She started to shake, and Marcus finally noticed that she wasn't dressed for the outdoors. He led her inside and sat her by the fire, the dog taking up a position at the front door. She looked up at him from her chair. "If what you say is true, then what can I do?"

"You'll have to leave."

"I can't leave! I have an inn to run!"

Marcus swept a hand at the room. "Not much of one, from what I can see."

She glared at him defensively, then bit her tongue. "And what of my husband?"

"He'll have to come with us too. Where is he?"

"He should be back shortly."

"Then you must pack what you need now. We'll leave as soon as he gets here."

She rose, still shivering and shaking from the cold and fear. "But where will we go?"

"Versailles. It's not far from here, and there's a Templar Commandry there. They'll be able to help. I'll escort you much of the way, and give you a message for the commander there. He knows me."

She sighed, her shoulders slumping. "Very well." She looked up at him. "But when my husband gets here, can we blame this on you? If he hears it was my loose tongue that got us in trouble, I'll never hear the end of it."

Marcus chuckled. "I shall accept full responsibility, madam, rest assured."

La Conciergerie Prison
Paris, Kingdom of France

Simon lay huddled in the corner, soaked with sweat as his body shook from the pain and dampness, and his head throbbed with a dull ache and occasional stabbing blindness.

He was at his breaking point.

He wasn't sure how long it had been. He guessed at least a month, perhaps longer, perhaps much longer. He hadn't seen even a beam of sunlight since he arrived, and was only guessing at the number of days based upon the number of times he had been fed, which he assumed was once a day.

Though there were days when he had discovered meals only enjoyed by the rats, the plate exchanged when a fresh one arrived. How many times that had happened without him knowing, he had no idea.

Perhaps it was months.

He was emaciated. He could feel it, the dark no protection against that particular horror, and his breathing was labored, his poor heart ready to fail from the constant torture and lack of proper meals. He was dying, and in fact, he suspected he had mere days left, if not hours. His only hope of surviving was to take Antoine's suggestion and confess.

Yet he still refused.

I will not confess to crimes I haven't committed, especially ones so heinous.

But wasn't it the same advice he had given

Antoine? Hadn't he told him to confess and beg for forgiveness? To barter his good name to gain his freedom?

Yet there was a difference. Antoine was guilty of his crime, though provoked. The advice was to admit to the crime, give an explanation for it, and to offer to make amends.

There was no sin in that.

But to confess to murder, when not guilty of it?

Never!

He sighed, trying to calm himself, missing the conversations with Antoine that had helped occupy his time these past several days. The fact he hadn't returned suggested that perhaps the man had taken his advice and been successful, though there was a worse possibility.

By admitting to his crime, he might have condemned himself to death, the sentence already carried out.

Simon shivered at the thought, his body racked with guilt, and he said a silent prayer for his friend.

The clang of the outer door no longer had his heart racing, no longer had him scrambling to prepare for another possible torture session. Instead, he simply listened for the telltale signs he was about to be fed.

That, he would move for. He had still heard nothing beyond confirmation word had gotten out about his plight, and though that should be enough, he desperately wanted confirmation that Marcus had received his message.

Then he could die in peace.

Then he could give in to the inevitable, and stop the fight to stay alive just one more day, waiting for that message.

The cell door next to him opened then slammed shut again, and Simon's eyes shot wide as someone shuffled on the other side. He repositioned near the hole, though kept his silence, waiting to hear the outer door to their cellblock shut once more.

It did.

"Antoine, is that you?"

"It is I, brother. I'm happy to hear you still live."

Simon smiled. "And I you. You were gone for so long, I thought perhaps you had taken my advice and it had worked."

Antoine chuckled. "Oh, I took your advice, all right, and it worked to a point."

"I don't understand."

"Do you remember I said the lady had a suitor?"

"Yes."

"Well, he came to see me, rather than the lady. And he was having none of my excuses. In fact, he ordered me tortured for my efforts."

"That heathen!"

"Indeed. And he watched the entire time! You wouldn't believe how much he enjoyed it, I tell you. A sick one, that Gilles Laurent is."

Simon's heart almost stopped. "What did you say his name was?"

"Gilles Laurent. At least I think that's what it was. I only heard it said once."

Simon rolled onto his back, trying to control his pounding heart. "But that's impossible! I mean, the coincidence! It simply can't be."

"What are you talking about?"

"Gilles Laurent is the one I was telling you about. He's the one who put me here, I'm sure!"

He could hear Antoine shuffling on the other side, his voice louder. "You had only ever said his first name. I never made the connection, Gilles being such a common name. What do you think it means?"

Simon's mind was racing and his headache was returning with a vengeance. What *did* it mean? There was no way this was a coincidence. He didn't believe in them, at least not ones as great as this. He could think of only two things. Either Antoine was lying about everything he had said over the past days, or he was telling the truth. If he were lying, then it would explain many things. How his wife had the same name as Roland's, how his son had the same name as Christian, and how the woman he happened to rob was being courted by his arch nemesis. And it also explained why Antoine had encouraged him to confess to the crimes.

My God!

Though there was another possibility. He was telling the truth. And if he were, then this was all a manipulation of them both. Perhaps the suitor wasn't Gilles at all, but someone else entirely. Perhaps Gilles had merely taken advantage of the situation. He obviously had pull at the prison to have him condemned here and tortured without end. In fact, it was probably Gilles standing behind him during so many of these sessions, taking great pleasure in seeing his enemy suffer. Gilles could have had Antoine put in the cell next to him, with the hopes that they would talk, and something of importance would be said that he could use against him. In fact, Gilles could be standing on the other side of the cell door, listening to this very conversation.

But that didn't make any sense. What could Gilles possibly hope to hear? He had all the evidence he needed to condemn him to death. He had the body, the witnesses, the past transgression. He had it all. He even had the attempted escape.

All more than enough to see him swing.

No, it made no sense.

And that left Simon with only one conclusion. Antoine was lying.

He stifled a gasp, trying to picture Gilles in his mind. Did he have all his fingers? Was he missing a finger as Antoine was? Could it be Gilles himself on the other side of the wall? His mouth went dry with the very idea of it.

But the voice. Surely, it was different.

Though he couldn't be certain. He had only heard Gilles speak the night he was arrested, and it was in confident, loud tones, not the whispered, tortured ones of a man condemned.

It couldn't be.

Could it?

"What is wrong, my friend? You say nothing."

Simon drew in a long, slow breath, debating what to say. Now that he knew at least some of the truth, that he was being played, either by Gilles alone, or by Antoine and Gilles both, he wasn't sure what to do. He desperately needed Antoine's company, and he could think of nothing that he could possibly say that would make his situation worse.

He smiled slightly.

If it were Gilles, perhaps he could provoke him into revealing himself, if he chose his words wisely.

"I'm sorry, my friend, but your words shocked me. I've been trying to figure out what it means, but I'm not sure. I must assume he's trying to manipulate us both."

"To what end? I'm a guilty man, and you're an innocent one already condemned to death. Why not just kill you and get it over with? Why all the trickery?"

Simon shook his head. "He was always that way. Even as a boy, he was manipulating things. Spreading lies, beating up smaller boys, even picking on girls. He was a horrible child."

"It doesn't sound like he's changed much."

"Indeed. Did I tell you about what happened the day he pushed Christian into the well?"

"Yes, my friend, you did. A horrible thing that was."

"Yes, but did I tell you *why* he pushed him?"

There was a pause. "No, I don't believe you did."

"It was because Gilles claimed to have hair between his legs, and we demanded proof, so he dropped his pants and revealed that he had only *one* hair."

"One!"

"Yes, a lone, solitary hair!"

Antoine started to laugh, a belly laugh so loud and so infectious, that Simon joined in, the painful experience exquisite though exhausting. He finally forced himself to stop, instead smiling at the continued laughter from the other side of the wall.

And it removed any doubt from his mind whether

Antoine was Gilles.

There was no way the man he had met a month ago would laugh so heartily at his own expense, not over such a humiliating event.

No, Antoine was not Gilles, and Simon was now having his doubts on whether Antoine was in on anything that might be going on. Would he dare laugh so long and so hard if he knew Gilles was listening in? He couldn't see it. There was no way, not if he knew the type of man Gilles truly was.

No, Antoine couldn't possibly think Gilles was listening.

But what did that mean? Did it mean that he was merely reporting back on their conversations?

Or was he innocent in all this?

But the names!

None of it explained those coincidences. Cateline and Christian. Both names from his own life. How could that possibly be?

It made no sense.

And again, he asked why it mattered.

He had his companion back, and anything he said wouldn't matter in the end.

For his end was near.

And assured.

Approaching Le Chesnay, Kingdom of France

Marcus let the horse lead the way as he tried to order his thoughts after seeing Mrs. Dubois and her husband safely on to Versailles. They had encountered no problems along the way, and as they neared the much bigger town, he had encountered another Templar Knight who had been happy to accompany them on the remainder of their journey.

But that was only one minor headache out of the way.

Unfortunately, there hadn't been much conversation, the couple clearly terrified and unwilling to share any more information than Mrs. Dubois already had. It was clear to him that she knew what was going on. In fact, it was clear to him that everyone in the town knew what was going on.

They were *all* scared.

And it had to be Gilles Laurent and his men. They were the only ones that seemed to wield any power, and would be the only ones with any official authority. And the fact that Gilles had so many men helping him made no sense, not for a town that size.

And a jail?

No, this man had clearly exceeded his authority, and the townsfolk were too scared to say anything about it.

But what was he doing with that authority that could so scare these people? Business appeared to be steady, at least from what he could see, and if highwaymen were indeed robbing those passing through, it must be a recent development, as word would get out and this would no longer be a preferred route through to Paris.

His eyes narrowed as he glanced about.

If it were a preferred route, then why was he now alone?

It could be a coincidence. With Paris so close, he suspected travel would happen closer to the end of the day, so that one could rest in one of the inns, then leave for Paris fresh in the morning, rather than try to kill one's time for the better part of a day in a small place that had little to offer in the way of entertainment.

Just coincidence.

If Gilles was involved with the highwaymen, he could be taking a cut of the profits, but if he had built the jail a couple of years ago, as Mr. Chastain had said, then this had been going on for some time, and there was no way that repeated attacks on travelers would go unnoticed, and unreported.

He would end up with nothing at all if the travelers through town dried up.

Though Gilles might be involved with the thievery taking place, he doubted this was what was going on. The townsfolk were scared, though doing well enough. If their businesses were suffering, and they knew it was because of his petty thievery, he would have sensed more anger and resentment, rather than what he had.

Had Simon stumbled onto whatever was going on? He doubted that. From what he could tell, he had been there mere hours before the arrest. Perhaps Roland had told him something, but again, what could

Simon have possibly done between that conversation and his arrest? By all reports, he had gone directly to his parents and remained there. And why would Roland tell him anything? Simon was a stranger after thirty years.

Though perhaps Simon's position as a Templar sergeant had emboldened the man.

Marcus sighed, shaking his head. Whatever had happened, he was certain was all related to Gilles, and until he could figure out what was going on, he had no hope of finding Simon.

He had to force the situation.

He had to cause Gilles to make a mistake.

And there was only one way he could think of to do that.

Rustling in the trees had him pausing in his thoughts, Tanya growling.

And this time there was no hesitation on the part of his assailants, half a dozen of them appearing within moments, four in front of him, blocking his way, and two behind, all armed with an assortment of arms, from axes to mallets, even a few with swords.

And only one with a bow.

Fools.

"We meet again, gentlemen. As I said before, I am a Templar, therefore have no money worth stealing."

The apparent leader stepped forward, beating the face of his mallet against the palm of his other hand. "We'll be taking that fine horse today. And the saddle. And anything else you've got on you."

Marcus smiled pleasantly as he swept his surcoat out of the way. "Then how will I travel? On foot?

Surely you don't expect me to do such a thing."

"No, Sir Marcus, we don't expect that you'll be doing much walking at all."

Marcus smiled. "So you know my name. Interesting."

The man paused for a moment, looking at the others, probably trying to figure out if he had let something slip. "Never mind all that. Get off the horse. Now!"

Marcus drew his sword and pointed it at the man with the bow. "Tanya, attack!"

She growled, leaping forward as Marcus urged his horse toward the leader. The man with the bow drew an arrow, then his eyes bulged with fear as he finally realized the massive canine had chosen him for her target. He dropped his bow and tried to run.

There was no point.

Tanya leaped on his back, her deadly jaws chomping at the nape of his neck as her weight brought him to the ground.

Marcus paid it no mind as he surged forward, leaning to his right slightly and swinging his blade, cleaving half the leader's head clean off. He continued forward, swinging again at another, then ducked as he spotted an axe whipping through the air toward him.

Disarming the man.

Recovering his position in the saddle, he ran down his target, then turned his horse.

"Tanya, break!"

The dog stepped back, her target whimpering, and Marcus pointed at the two who had covered the rear. "Attack!"

She dutifully leaped into action, and he had to wonder at times whether she knew the seriousness of what she was doing, or if this was simply good fun to her.

A sword was raised in trembling hands to challenge him as Tanya's targets turned to flee. Marcus rode the man through, an attempt to parry never provided.

With the four men down, he whistled and Tanya turned, happily racing back to his side. He dismounted and stepped over to Tanya's first target and flipped him over with a boot.

"Who sent you?"

"N-no one."

"You're going to die here today. Wouldn't you rather die knowing you had told the truth?"

The man stared up at him, his entire body shaking, the fear of death in his eyes. "With all I've done, it wouldn't make any difference."

Marcus sighed. "So be it." He raised his sword, grabbing it upside down by the hilt, then dropped it hard into the man's chest, piercing the ribcage until coming to a stop when it reached the frozen ground. He placed a boot on the corpse, the heart pierced, and pulled his sword free.

Tanya sniffed the now still man, as if disappointed she no longer had anyone to play with.

And Marcus took a moment to pray for their souls, though he too was certain it would make no difference.

Templar Commandry
Versailles, Kingdom of France

David spotted the Templar flag first, the red cross on crisp white always a welcome sight. He only prayed that there was news on Simon, though he doubted it. If their sergeant were indeed in La Conciergerie Prison as Thomas had said, and had been there for over a month, he was likely already dead, or beyond hope of rescue.

Whoever would condemn an innocent man to that long in prison, subject to torture, had no intention of ever letting him out.

And the Order wasn't about to invade the prison and risk challenging the King, a king that was no friend to the Templars, not with the amount of money he owed them.

"I'm looking forward to a good meal and a hot bath."

David nodded at the younger Jeremy. "Me too. It's been a long ride, though I fear we may not have any time for luxuries."

Jeremy grunted. "You're probably right. I still think it was wise to bypass Paris."

David agreed. With the extra provisions provided by Lady Joanne and Beatrice, they had debated the necessity of stopping at the Templar headquarters and reporting Simon's situation. Past experience told them they could end up waiting hours for an audience, and they had both agreed little would probably be done, as there was little that *could* be done.

They had agreed that pushing through to Versailles, where Marcus had said he would send any messages, would be the place to start, and from what they had been told, it was on the way to Le Chesnay, the town where the records Jeremy had retrieved indicated Simon had been born.

They both dismounted and tied up their horses before entering the solid structure, the flag snapping overhead in a brisk, wintery wind.

Jeremy shivered. "It's days like these that make me miss the desert."

"You've obviously not been long back."

David bowed to the Templar Knight sitting behind a simple desk in the center of the room, piled with papers. "Only a few months, sir."

"The same for myself." The knight pointed at a long scar on his face. "I'm afraid this ended my time in service to our Lord in the Holy Land."

"It is an honor to be in the presence of a true warrior."

The man bowed his head. "I am Sir Piers de Vichiers. And you are?"

"Sir, I am David, this is Jeremy, squires to Sir Marcus de Rancourt."

"Ahh, Sir Marcus! Yes, I met him recently. Has he found your sergeant?"

David shook his head. "I'm afraid we have not yet had word from him on the matter beyond that he arrived here. *We*, however, received concerning news, and decided it was best to come here at once."

Sir Piers seemed genuinely concerned, beckoning them to sit in two chairs in front of his desk. They sat, and the man leaned forward. "Tell me, what is this

161

news?"

"We received word from a trusted source that Simon is being held in La Conciergerie Prison, and being tortured."

Piers leaned back, his eyes wide. "Whatever for?"

"We don't know. All we know is he is being held there, and may not have long to live, if he even lives at all."

"Have you reported this?"

"Not yet. We are here to do that now, then find our master so as to warn him."

"Warn him? Of what?"

David's heart pounded with fear for Marcus. "Sir, Simon went to meet his family, and we never heard back from him. It was our master's belief that something happened to him immediately upon arriving in his hometown, as he didn't even have time to send a message through here, as he had promised. If something did indeed happen to him, and he is now in prison being tortured, then there is obviously great danger facing our master, and he has no idea of it. We must warn him at once."

Piers' head slowly bobbed. "Agreed, you must. I will send word by urgent messenger to Paris at once about your sergeant, though I fear little can be done beyond official inquiries to the King's Court, and with relations the way they are, I doubt any satisfaction will be found."

David frowned. "I'm afraid we came to the same conclusion."

Piers pulled out a blank piece of paper, his hand rapidly scribbling a message. "There is no harm in trying, and perhaps if the powers that be know that *we* know Simon is there, it might give them pause before they do him any more harm."

David exchanged an excited glance with Jeremy, this something that hadn't occurred to him. Then regret swept through him as he realized they could have perhaps relieved Simon's suffering far sooner if they had stopped in Paris.

"And you two should go to Le Chesnay. It's an hour north of here, on the road you just came in on. And be careful. There have been reports of highwaymen, though none that have suggested Templars have been accosted as of yet."

David frowned. "Perhaps Simon was the first."

Piers shook his head. "Highwaymen don't have Templar sergeants placed in prison. Whatever your sergeant stumbled into, has nothing to do with common thieves." He snapped his fingers and a boy rushed over.

"Sir?"

"Two fresh horses for these men, and supplies for two days' ride."

"At once, sir."

The boy disappeared and Piers smiled at their puzzled expressions. "It's only one hour from here, but just in case you don't receive a friendly welcome, perhaps a little extra food and water might be needed."

David bowed his head, as did Jeremy. "Thank you, sir. A wise precaution."

Piers finished writing his letter, then folded the paper and sealed it. He held it up and a man emerged from the shadows. "For the headquarters in Paris. It is urgent. Wait for a reply. I don't want this one ignored."

"Yes, sir."

The messenger rushed out the front door, and David felt a surge of pride in the organization he served, as an already prepared horse was mounted and immediately galloped away.

Paris would know before the end of the day, and perhaps Simon might find some reprieve.

Bailiff's Delegate's Office
Le Chesnay, Kingdom of France

Marcus sat in the heart of what was likely enemy territory. In fact, he was certain of it. He didn't trust Gilles Laurent at all. Everything suggested he was behind all of this, yet he had not one shred of proof of anything beyond an unfriendly demeanor.

None of which was visible at this moment, instead a broad smile on display.

"Have you lost respect for your friend?"

Marcus eyed him. "Why would you ask such a thing?"

Gilles jerked a thumb over his shoulder, at the wall beyond which the burned-out jail lay. "Your friend's body still lies in the snow and ashes. I should think you would have claimed him by now and had him buried with honor."

"All in good time." Marcus shifted in his chair, resting an elbow on one of the arms. "I would ask why he was your prisoner."

Gilles' eyes widened. "You haven't been told? I'm surprised at that. I would have thought Mr. and Mrs. Chastain would have filled you in, at least."

"I've heard many things. I'd like to hear the official version, from the King's representative for this town."

Gilles' chest swelled at the mention of his position, the man clearly enamored with the power and prestige it granted him. "I arrested him that night because he killed a witness to a crime from our childhood."

165

"Mr. Roland Villeneuve."

"Yes. According to witnesses, he met him almost immediately upon arriving in town, a meeting was arranged at Roland's house for a very short while later, and Simon went inside, where he eventually ran Roland through with his sword, then fled to his parents' home."

"And how do you know it was him? Why couldn't he have been killed by someone else after he left?"

"We have a man who witnessed him leaving in a suspicious manner. The man went inside the home out of concern for Roland, and found him dead. There can be no doubt."

"And this witness is?"

"Of no importance to you. Simon was guilty, of that, I can assure you."

"But surely a man has the right to face his accuser."

"He forfeited that right when he tried to escape, and got himself killed."

Marcus kept his expression neutral, rather than give any suggestion to the man that he knew this to be a lie. "And the crime that Roland witnessed?"

Gilles made himself more comfortable, as if he were about to enjoy what he was going to say. "When we were children, Simon beat a boy and pushed him into the river. The boy fell through the ice and drowned. Simon ran away, never to be seen again."

"That doesn't sound like Simon."

Gilles grunted. "He was a vicious one back then. Full of hate and jealousy. He beat Christian for some perceived slight. What, I can't remember anymore. Nothing worth dying over, I assure you."

"And then he just ran away."

Gilles shifted in his chair, shrugging slightly as he tried to appear modest for what Marcus was sure was a well-practiced lie. "I actually did fight him, to try and stop him from getting away. After all, I was the son of a man who held the position I now occupy. Unfortunately, he managed to get away. That was when I guess he met up with your people."

Marcus sat for a moment, processing everything. The story just spun by Gilles about their childhood was definitely plausible. Children did stupid things in fits of anger, and sometimes the consequences were dire. What was troubling was the fact he had known Simon for over twenty years, and there had never been any mention of this incident. If innocent, Marcus would have thought a word or two on the matter might have been spoken over the years, yet nothing had.

Though despite the fact Marcus couldn't speak to what happened back then, as he didn't know Simon the child, he did know the man. And that man had told his parents that he hadn't killed the boy all those years ago. And the Simon he knew now didn't lie.

Never.

And that meant he didn't kill Christian all those years ago, so had absolutely no reason to kill Roland a month ago, for Roland was the only other witness who could point a finger at the person truly responsible, sitting across from him now.

He pressed Gilles.

Gently.

"But why kill Roland? And so quickly?"

Gilles shrugged. "I suppose because he was the

only other witness, besides me, to the crime."

Marcus nodded thoughtfully for show. "And you think he would have come after you next?"

Gilles leaned forward. "Absolutely! Fortunately for me, his crime was discovered quickly, and we were able to take him at his parents' home without a fight."

Marcus' eyebrows rose slightly. "Without? That doesn't sound like a guilty man to me."

Gilles smiled. "There were five of us."

Marcus smiled bigger. "Then you are lucky. I've seen him take on ten, and win. Fortunately for you, he's now dead."

"Yes, indeed."

Marcus took a slight risk. "And you have no doubt the man who died in the fire was Simon?"

Gilles folded his arms. "Absolutely none. All prisoners were accounted for." He eyed him. "Why? Do you have doubts?"

"No, I'm sure I don't, though I did speak to someone who swore he heard prisoners being transferred about the time of the fire."

Gilles' nostrils flared, a hint of fury in his eyes at the mention someone had informed on him. "We were planning on transferring someone when your sergeant attempted escape. After he died, we took the survivors to another town, since we no longer had facilities."

"What town?"

Gilles stared at him for a moment. "Excuse me?"

"What town did you transfer them to?"

"I hardly think it matters."

Marcus smiled. "Please, settle my curiosity,

otherwise it will drive me quite insane, and I'll be forced to find out for myself."

"Again, it doesn't matter, and I can assure you, it is no business of yours."

Marcus held up his hands and shrugged. "If it's a secret, then far be it for me to pry."

Gilles unfolded his arms and rose. "I think you've wasted enough of my time."

Marcus remained seated. "You said you were there that day, when young Christian was killed."

"I was."

"And you would swear to our Lord Himself that Simon was the one responsible."

Gilles shifted from one foot to the other. "I would."

Marcus rose. "Very well, perhaps I didn't know my sergeant as well as I had thought."

"Evidently." Gilles opened the door. "Now be off with you, I have business to attend to."

"Of course." Marcus paused in the doorway. "Oh, there is one more thing. The original reason I came here. I was accosted on the way into town by six men. You'll find the bodies of four of them on the road to Versailles."

Gilles eyes flared, his face getting a little pinker. "I'll have my men check it out. I trust you weren't hurt?"

"Not a scratch, thank you for your concern." Marcus bowed. "Now, I'll let you get on with your day." He stepped off the porch and mounted his horse before Gilles could say anything further. Though he had said enough. Gilles had been surprised to see him, and was angry at the news of the deaths. Which Marcus could only interpret in one way.

They had to be his men.

He slowly made his way toward the Chastain residence as he gathered his thoughts. He considered himself quite good at reading people, and was convinced that almost every single word out of Gilles' mouth was a lie. He had no doubt Gilles was the one who killed Christian, then framed Simon for it, which is probably why he ran away for fear of not being believed. He also had no doubt that it was Gilles or one of his men that killed Roland, and framed Simon.

Even if he was mistaken, and Simon had killed Christian years ago, Simon was a man of God now. If he had indeed been responsible, the last thing he would do would be to kill the witnesses. If anything, he would turn himself in and beg for mercy, then be satisfied with whatever justice was meted out, including death.

That was the Simon he knew, not the panicked little boy who ran away rather than face the consequences of actions that might not have even been his own.

A horse whinnied and he glanced over his shoulder to see Gilles sticking his cane in a loop on his saddle, his horse provisioned for a journey of at least several hours.

I wonder where he's going.

He spotted the older woman who had been willing to speak to him, staring after Gilles, then spitting on the ground as he rode out of sight. In fact, most of the townsfolk he could see, appeared to be standing a little taller.

These poor people.

He had to figure out what was going on, beyond just what was happening with Simon. Even if it turned out his sergeant was dead, these people needed help, and as a knight, it was his duty to see justice prevail.

He just had no idea how he might accomplish that.

He dismounted and approached the woman, bowing slightly, remembering how much she had enjoyed his first greeting, delivering it again with a smile. "Milady."

She tossed her head back and roared with laughter, the others joining in. "And what brings you to my little corner of the market once again, Sir Knight?"

He made a point of looking over her baked goods, his stomach rumbling as he tried to recall the last time he ate. Templars relied upon the Order, or the charity of others, forbidden from carrying more than four deniers unless there was good need.

Unfortunately, him off on his own, investigating the disappearance of his sergeant, and not on official business, would not constitute good need.

She handed him a roll. "Eat. You look famished."

"I couldn't possibly, Milady. I haven't anything for which to pay you."

She lowered her voice, pressing it into his palm. "You've caused some headaches for that one"—she jutted her chin toward the building he had just left—"which is payment enough for me."

He smiled, taking the roll and bowing slightly. "I thank you kindly. May the good Lord watch over you and your household, and keep them safe."

"A blessing from a Templar. Too bad you weren't here a month ago to offer it."

171

Marcus bit into the crusty roll, savoring the flavors exploding in his mouth, the woman definitely a talent. As he chewed, he nodded after Gilles. "Any idea where he's going?"

She shrugged. "All I know is we're better off when he's not here."

Marcus took a chance. "Why is that?"

"You do ask a lot of questions, don't you? If you're not careful, you could end up like your sergeant. I fear he may have asked too many questions as well."

Marcus frowned. "From my understanding, he barely had time to."

"Aye, this is true, though perhaps fear of what he might ask is what led to his demise."

"About what happened when he was a child?"

The woman eyed him. "You know of that?"

"I do, though I've heard different versions. Were you there?"

"Not at the killing, but I was at the church when we found out about it. Half the town was." She shook her head. "I never believed what Gilles said of your Simon, not, that is, until Roland confirmed the story." She sighed. "I'll never forget that day. It was a big thing in these parts. A young lad missing, another accused of murdering him. Gilles was feted as a hero, if you can believe that!"

"Why?"

"Well, he tried to stop Simon from running away, didn't he?"

Marcus pressed. "Did he?"

"According to him and Roland, Gilles wrestled with Simon, but Simon got the better of him and escaped, though not before tearing Gilles' prized shirt."

There were a few nods from the older vendors within earshot.

"Prized shirt?" It was the first new piece of information he had heard after several retellings of the story.

"Yes, the boy was so proud of it. His mother had bought it in Paris just the week before. It was the first day he had been allowed to wear it. For church, you know." She chuckled. "I swear that woman was more upset that it had been torn than she was that a boy might be dead."

"And they never found the body?"

She frowned. "No. Swept away in the river."

"I see." He stared in the direction Gilles had left. "I wonder where he's going. He had provisions for a not insignificant ride."

She shrugged. "Don't care, as long as he's gone." She tapped her chin then looked about, as if to make sure they were alone. She leaned closer and lowered her voice. "I'll tell you this. Since your friend died in the fire, he's been leaving several times a week at this time, then doesn't return until dusk."

Marcus' eyebrows rose. "So often?"

"Yes. And since you've returned? He goes every day."

"And this is unusual for him? To leave on business so frequently?"

"So frequently, yes. He likes to keep a close watch on things, never liking to let things out of his sight."

Marcus' head slowly bobbed. "Interesting." He

bowed, then held up what little remained of his roll. "Thank you for your time, Milady, and for the alms." His eyes swept the street. "Now, do you know any place that might serve me?"

She grunted, then jerked her head toward the shop behind her. "If you promise to not ask any more questions, I'll feed you. No one else will in these parts." She shuffled from the table set up out front and through the door. He tied up his horse and indicated for Tanya to stay, then followed her inside, the warmth from a baker's oven greeting him.

He took a seat at a table in the back as the old woman dished out a healthy serving of stew, placing it in front of him along with a loaf of bread. He smiled. "A meal fit for a king."

"You deserve it, I'm sure."

He bowed his head. "Thank you." He tore off a piece of the bread, dipping it into the bowl before taking a bite, savoring every chew, each swallow reminding him of home. Not home in the Holy Land, but home on the farm, and the delicious meals prepared by the various women that had helped them over the past months.

"Can I ask you something?"

She frowned at him. "I thought we had an agreement."

"We did, but now that no one can hear us, there is something I must know. Please feel free not to answer, but if I didn't take the opportunity to at least ask, I'd be remiss in my duties."

She placed a cup of milk on the table. "Ask your question, but don't expect a response."

"Why is everyone so scared around here?"

She eyed him. "You've noticed that, have you?"

"I have, though you don't seem afraid."

She dropped into a chair across from him. "I was, until my nephew was killed. I realized then that I didn't care to live anymore. Not in a world such as this."

Marcus regarded her. "I'm sorry to hear that. How did he die?"

She stared at him, saying nothing for a moment. "If we're to believe our friend the Bailiff's Delegate, your sergeant, Simon, killed him."

Roland Villeneuve's Residence
Le Chesnay, Kingdom of France

"I haven't touched anything since they took him away."

Marcus examined the humble home from the doorway, the old lady, who he had learned was named Mathilde Villeneuve, granting his wish to see the scene of the murder his sergeant had been accused of, though not before finishing the best meal he had partaken of since leaving the farm.

"Where is your nephew buried?"

"Out back."

"And his family?"

"Gone. They left to stay with her family in Chartres. I fear I may never see them again at my age."

He frowned, stepping deeper inside. "What will become of the place?"

She shrugged. "Someone will take it over eventually. It's good land."

Marcus eyed the pool of blood where Roland had evidently bled out, a large void in the shape of part of his torso indicating he hadn't moved for some time after being stabbed, the blood drying in place.

He spotted something, his eyes narrowing, and he held the torch out in front of him as he took a knee, careful not to disturb anything. "It looks like someone stood over him and watched him bleed to death."

Mathilde shuffled up beside him, and he held out a hand to stop her before she stepped into the dried blood. "What makes you say that?"

He pointed at two voids in the blood, only feet from where Roland would have lain. "These are footprints, side by side without any blood under them. That means whoever was standing here, was doing so before the blood reached his feet."

"How do you figure?"

"If he stepped into the blood after it was already there, then there would be blood *under* the footprints. But there's none, just bare floor."

Mathilde smiled. "You're a smart man, Sir Knight."

He chuckled. "I am but what God made me." He moved the torch closer, spotting something else to the right of the two footprints, another small void in the blood. "I wonder what this is."

Mathilde bent over and stared, then stood back up. "My eyes aren't what they used to be. I can't even see what you're looking at."

Marcus rose. "Perhaps it is nothing." He slowly walked about the home, searching for anything out of the ordinary, but found nothing. There were no signs that there was a struggle of any kind, everything neat and orderly, Roland's wife clearly taking pride in an orderly home.

He ended his search at the door. "I think I've seen all I need to see, thank you."

Mathilde stared up at him. "Did it help?"

Marcus pursed his lips then nodded. "I believe so."

"So, did your friend kill my Roland?"

Marcus shook his head, certain for the first time since he had arrived that his friend was completely innocent of the crime. "No."

"You sound certain."

"I am." He pointed at the footprints. "Those footprints are far too small to be my sergeant's. Whoever did this was a much slighter man, or at least a man with small feet." He sighed in relief as he spoke the words, staring at the footprints. "This convinces me, beyond a doubt, that Simon had nothing to do with this murder." He looked at the old woman. "And if he didn't, then he likely had nothing to do with the murder of Christian when he was a child."

"Then who did it? Who killed my Roland?"

"Someone who doesn't want us to know who the guilty party is from thirty years ago."

"You mean…" She seemed terrified to say it.

Marcus nodded. "Can you think of another?"

Mathilde shook her head. "But if it is him, then your life is in grave danger."

Marcus frowned. "As I fear is yours, my good lady, for showing me this."

She grunted. "If the truth will come out because of what I've done here today, then I would gladly give my life." She grabbed his arm. "I will pray for you tonight, young man, for I fear your only hope of surviving is with His help."

Entering Le Chesnay, Kingdom of France

David frowned as they entered Le Chesnay, the apparent hometown of their sergeant, Simon.

And an unfriendly one at that.

"Do you get the sense we're not welcome here?"

David grunted at Jeremy's observation. "These people are about as friendly as the sergeant is in the morning."

"I guess we know where he gets it from."

David chuckled. "If this was the kind of welcome he received, no wonder there was trouble. The sergeant doesn't take kindly to rudeness."

"Nor Sir Marcus. Neither, I think, would make good fits here. Thank God Crécy-la-Chapelle isn't like this."

"Agreed. Perhaps we've got it better there than we thought."

Jeremy frowned. "So, you've been having second thoughts?"

David nodded, his stomach flipping at the idea of voicing concerns that went against what the master wanted. "I have. Haven't we all?"

Jeremy rolled his eyes. "I thought it was obvious. That's why Simon left, wasn't it? And did you see the master's face when you made that little joke? One would think you stabbed him in the heart."

David sighed. "More like the back." He shook his head. "We all agreed to stay, and we made that decision freely."

"Did we? He is our master, after all. We are supposed to serve him."

"Yes, but we're not slaves. He gave us the opportunity to leave, and the Order would never have questioned us wanting to leave his side and rejoin the active forces. We stayed out of loyalty to him."

Jeremy shifted in his saddle. "Yes, this is true, but now with time, I think we're all wondering if that was the right choice. Certainly Simon was."

"I had the impression there was something more going on with him. More than just the new life. Did you see the way he looked at the boys? There was something there, in his eyes. As if he was in pain."

Jeremy's head bobbed slowly. "Yes, I did notice he was different the past couple of months, but I always assumed it was general unhappiness at the new life."

David sighed. "Do you miss it?"

"Miss what?"

"The old life. In the Holy Land, fighting the Saracens, living with our brothers of the Order?"

Jeremy frowned. "Some days, immensely, other days, not at all. And I must admit, as time passes, the latter outnumbers the former. While part of me misses the work we were doing there, I've come to realize that we are doing God's work here, too. Think about it. What did we actually do there? We're squires. We weren't fighting unless we had to. We were following Sir Marcus and Simon, carrying spare equipment, and making sure *they* were able to fight."

"True, though I lost count of how many times we saved their asses."

Jeremy grinned. "They'll never admit to it! I'm not trying to trivialize what we were usually doing. It was of critical importance. But most of what we were doing wasn't glorious. No more glorious than shoveling dung at the farm."

David chuckled. "I think we need to try and delegate those duties to the boys."

Jeremy tossed his head back, laughing. "Definitely! The next time they quarrel, hand them each a pitchfork." He sighed. "I like the children. I never thought I would, but I do. It reminds me of when I was a boy, before I left to join the Order." He frowned, his eyes staring off into the distance. "I miss those days. I can see why Simon would want to come back and revisit them."

David frowned. "And look where it got him." He jabbed a finger at Jeremy. "When we find Sir Marcus, and get Simon out of prison, I vote we all return to the farm and never leave it again."

Jeremy laughed. "So then the decision has been made? We remain farmers?"

David smiled. "I guess it has. You know, just talking about it freely, and realizing I'm not alone in how I'm feeling, makes me more confident that we made the right choice. I can't explain it, but I suddenly am fine with giving up the life of constant battle and prayer, for a life where we farm the land like the average man, and protect those women and children." He inhaled deeply, sitting a little higher in the saddle. "I think I could face the Lord, when it's all over, and feel confident he would be pleased with my decision."

Jeremy nodded. "I as well." He looked about. "Now, where do you think we're going to find Sir Marcus?"

David shrugged. "I say we find out where Simon's

family lives, and start there." He guided his horse toward one of the street vendors packing up for the day, dusk upon them. "Excuse me, sir. Where might we find the Chastain family?"

The man's eyes went wide, then wider still when he noticed their brown tunics and red crosses. He pointed in the direction they had been heading. "Cross the bridge just out of town. It's the first farm on the left."

David bowed his head to the man. "Thank you, sir." He urged his horse on a little faster, Jeremy at his side, and as they approached the outskirts of the town, he heard something on the cold wind and brought his steed to a halt, cocking an ear. "What was that?"

"I think it was a woman's scream." Jeremy pointed back from where they had just come. "I think it came from back there."

David urged his horse forward as he drew his sword, turning to Jeremy. "In the months we've been back, I think we've seen more action than we would have in the Holy Land!"

Jeremy laughed. "A simpler life, with action too!"

David smiled as the wind swept through his hair, the muscles of the mighty beast he straddled pulsing under him, and a contented sigh escaped as the energy brought on by the thrill of battle surged through him.

Staying is absolutely the right choice.

Mathilde Villeneuve Residence
Le Chesnay, Kingdom of France

Mathilde lifted the boiling pot of water off the fire, then poured some into her cup, the mix of herbs and spices beginning to steep, her tisane soon to be ready. She sat in the same chair she had for decades, taking over the family business from her parents years ago, and never having moved out.

She had never taken a husband, and it was her mother's greatest regret, and a terrible disappointment to her father. Though it wasn't for lack of trying on their part. They had searched far and wide for a suitor, but everyone that came, left almost as quickly.

For she wasn't an attractive girl.

She knew it, and her parents knew it, though thankfully they had never said anything to her.

She hadn't realized how ugly she was until she first saw her own reflection in a pot of water as she carried it for her mother.

And it had terrified her. She had cried for days, finally understanding why the mean children were always teasing her.

She learned later in life that something had gone wrong in the birth, her head getting twisted or something, that had left it misshapen. This had set her jaw and nose off, and her ears at different heights. As she got older, these things grew slightly less pronounced. She grew her hair long and kept it over her ears so no one could notice, and she kept her head at a tilt that aligned things to appear almost normal to

183

those who might glance at her casually, but it wasn't until true old age had settled in, that no one paid it any mind anymore, and she could finally stop worrying about it.

Though she never looked at herself in the water, or on a shiny surface, ever again.

And no man had ever beheld her with desire in his eyes. If she had ever managed to have a child, it truly would have been the Immaculate Conception once again.

She had felt sorry for herself for much of her life, certainly the first half, and especially after her parents had died together one winter, leaving her completely alone. She had an older brother who had a wonderful wife, but they too were taken that same winter, along with too large a portion of the town, some disease that she never understood having killed so many.

Roland had survived, her only living blood relation besides his children.

At least until a month ago.

Now he was gone, horribly, and his family lived at least a days' ride away, which might as well be on the other side of the Kingdom for all it would do her, a woman of her age never one to make such a journey.

She was alone.

She rose, retrieving her tisane, then sat back down by the fire, adjusting her blanket before taking a sip. She smiled, closed her eyes, and sighed. Leaning her head back, she sought the Lord in the Heaven above, and prayed for Him to take her soon, for she no longer had any desire to live.

The door flew open, nearly causing her to spill her hot tisane as a scream erupted. Two men stood in the doorway, and she recognized them as part of Gilles' contingent. She adjusted herself, determined to take up with the Lord His method of answering her prayer when she arrived.

She stared at the uninvited guests. "So, you've come to kill me, have you?"

The largest stepped closer. "Our master would like to know what you told the Templar."

A burst of air erupted from between her lips. "Nothing that is of your concern. But I'll tell you this! He knows that the Simon boy had nothing to do with the murder of my Roland. What do you think your master will have to say about that?"

The man sneered, drawing his sword. "I think he won't care in the slightest. A Templar Knight is of no concern to him. A Templar has no authority here, and my master does."

"Your master has overreached, and one of these days, that long neck he's stuck out is going to find itself severed from the body it is attached to. Mark my words, when that day comes, I'll be dancing beside his dead corpse, and cheering as they string up those who did his dirty work!"

"I can assure you that will never happen."

"Oh, and why is that?"

"Because you'll be long dead before that day ever arrives."

He raised his sword over his right shoulder and swung. Mathilde closed her eyes, her lips rapidly reciting the Lord's Prayer when a snarling growl filled the room. A man cried out in agony and terror, and Mathilde opened her eyes to see a large black dog latched onto her attacker's arm.

185

A groan from his partner went almost unnoticed as a shadowy figure rushed into her small home, the sound of a sword withdrawing from something simply causing more confusion as she tried to figure out what was happening.

Then her assailant's head separated from his body, dropping to the floor with a thud, rolling back toward the other man, now in a heap in the doorway. The headless corpse finally collapsed unceremoniously to the floor in front of her, the dog letting go of the arm, finally giving her a clear view of her savior.

"Sir Knight!"

"Milady, are you all right?"

She frowned at him. "I was about to be."

His eyes narrowed. "I don't understand."

She batted her hand at him, deciding explaining her life's story and desire to die, inappropriate at a time such as this. For whatever reason, the good Lord had decided this knight should stop her prayer from being answered.

Unfortunate.

The dog growled, bristling as it pointed its snout at the now gaping doorway. Marcus turned, his sword ready as the sound of horses approaching at high speed grew louder. They came to a halt and she heard two distinct thuds as their riders dismounted.

Then the panting of the dog as she happily trotted outside, apparently to greet the new arrivals.

Marcus frowned. "What kind of guard dog are you?"

"Tanya!" called someone from outside, and she noticed Marcus visibly relax, his sword lowering, his shoulders straightening. "What are you doing here,

186

girl?"

Marcus sheathed his sword. "I could ask you two the same question."

"Sir Marcus?" Two young men rushed inside, all smiles, and hugs were exchanged. "We feared the worst. Thank the Lord you're all right!"

Marcus regarded them, it evident to Mathilde that he was both displeased and pleased. "So, again I ask, why are you here and not at the farm, protecting the women and children as I ordered?"

The youngest smacked the older one's arm with the back of his hand. "David made me come with him."

David stared at his comrade. "Jeremy and I *both* felt it was necessary." He turned back to Marcus. "Sir, Thomas Durant came to the farm several days ago, with news of Simon."

This excited Marcus, all trace of anger vanquished. "What news? Is he alive?"

"He's being held prisoner in La Conciergerie Prison. Has been for over a month."

Marcus cursed, then stared up at the ceiling for a moment, the pious man probably apologizing to the Lord. "So that's where they took him. But why?"

"Apparently, he's being tortured. The woman who saw him said she felt he was near death. With Thomas confirming something had happened to Simon almost immediately upon arrival, we felt it was best to come here in case you needed help." David looked at the bodies still bleeding out on the floor. "It looks like you don't."

Marcus chuckled. "I've been handling myself quite nicely, thank you, but I'm glad you're here. Much has happened since I arrived, but first, what of Simon? What action have you taken?"

"We informed the commander in Versailles—"

"Sir Piers?"

"Yes. He immediately dispatched a message to Paris, with instructions to wait for an answer, though he wasn't confident much could be done."

Marcus shook his head. "I fear he might be right."

Mathilde noticed the blood continuing to spread, and muttered a curse, not bothering to apologize. She pointed at the bodies. "If you three are going to yammer, then why don't you first get these two things out of my house, and I'll prepare you a meal."

Marcus bowed apologetically. "Of course, Milady." He motioned toward the new arrivals. "May I present my squires, David and Jeremy."

Both boys bowed with flourishes.

"Mrs. Villeneuve has helped me in my quest to discover the truth behind what has happened here."

"Not Missus. I never married."

Marcus bowed again. "I apologize for the false assumption."

"No need to apologize." She gestured toward the new arrivals. "But if either of these two fine young specimens is looking for a wife, I'm available." She roared in laughter at their expressions of near horror, Marcus covering his own grin with his hand. He pointed at the bodies and flicked his wrist toward the door, David and Jeremy springing into action and removing them one at a time as she retrieved a bucket. She handed it to the youngest. "The well is out back. Keep filling it until you've washed the blood away."

"Yes, madam."

"I prefer, 'Milady.'" She howled with laughter at the confused expressions on both their faces, Marcus joining in at their expense. He turned to her as the young ones left.

"I think it's best we stay with you tonight, just in case."

"Oh, the scandal that will cause! The town will talk, I assure you!"

Marcus flushed, stammering out his words. "Umm, ahh, well, maybe, umm, perhaps we shouldn't."

She cackled at him. "I'm just having fun with you. Let them talk! Perhaps I'll have a little fun with *them* over it!"

Marcus' cheeks flushed, clearly embarrassed at the suggestion. The poor man was probably afflicted as she was, though by choice instead of punishment.

She patted him on the arm then her jaw dropped. She pointed at where the dog had walked through the blood. "Look! You were right! She stepped in the blood and you can tell it was already there!" She patted him on the cheek as the other two returned. "You are a smart boy, aren't you, Sir Knight?"

He flushed, even more when he saw his two squires grinning in the doorway. "Don't you two have work to do?"

Mathilde Villeneuve Residence
Le Chesnay, Kingdom of France

Marcus sat on the floor with his back against the wall next to the fire, David and Jeremy in front of him, their job of cleaning up the blood done, too many bucketsful of water needed to wash away the aftermath of the fight through the floorboards. Mathilde had insisted on preparing them a meal, and none refused. She was in the room next door, where her bakery was, hard at work in the late hours of the night. If he didn't know she was taking such great pleasure in doing so, he would have felt guilty about it.

"Here's what I know so far. When Simon was a child, there was apparently a fight. Simon was accused of pushing a child named Christian into the river. The boy fell through the ice and died."

Jeremy grunted. "Doesn't sound like Simon."

Marcus agreed. "No, it doesn't, but remember, he was a child back then, so anything is possible. There were two other people there. One was a boy named Roland, our good host's nephew, and another boy named Gilles Laurent, whose father was the Bailiff's Delegate for the area at the time."

"Not a good witness to have speaking against you," muttered David.

"Exactly. Gilles told the entire town that Simon had killed Christian, and that he fought with Simon to try and prevent him from escaping, but failed. Roland backed up the story, and Simon ran away, never to return."

David frowned. "Let me guess, that's not what actually happened."

Marcus nodded. "According to Simon's parents, Simon denied that version of events when he returned a month ago, and said that Gilles had actually been the one who pushed the boy, and that he threatened to kill Roland if he told the truth."

Jeremy sighed. "And with him being the Delegate's son, he never stood a chance."

"Exactly. Apparently, when Simon arrived, he encountered Roland within—"

David raised a finger. "How could he possibly have known it was him after all these years?"

"Bright red hair, apparently."

Jeremy exchanged a nod with David. "I could see that. It's rare enough."

"They met in Roland's home, then Simon left for his parents. Roland was then murdered, and Simon was arrested later that night by Gilles for the murder. During the middle of the night, according to Gilles, Simon died in a fire at the town's jail, a fire he started while trying to escape. He even showed me a burned body, claiming it was Simon."

David grunted. "Well, we know that's a lie, since Simon is in La Conciergerie Prison."

Jeremy agreed. "Which calls into question everything this Gilles character said. Can we prove Simon didn't murder Roland?" He held up his hands. "Not that I think he did, of course!"

Marcus nodded. "I can. Our host let me into Roland's home. It had been left untouched since the murder. There are footprints in the blood. Voids, as if the person who murdered Roland stood and watched him bleed out, rather than stepped into the blood. The blood flowed around his feet."

Jeremy grinned. "You *are* a smart boy, aren't you?"

Marcus gave him a look and David stifled a snort. "As I was saying, there are two distinct footprints, and they are far too small to be Simon's."

"The man does have big feet," agreed David.

"Yes, and a huge—"

Marcus stabbed a finger at the air between them. "Remember, we are guests in this house."

"A huge what?"

Cackling came from the obviously thin walls, and all three of them joined in for a moment before Marcus resumed relaying what he knew to this point. "So, I'm confident Simon didn't murder Roland, I knew he hadn't died in the fire, but I couldn't be sure he was still alive until now, and your revelation might just give us another piece of the puzzle."

David leaned forward. "What's that?"

"Our host has informed me that Gilles has been leaving several times a week for six to seven hours at a time, since Simon supposedly died. And every day since I arrived. Apparently, he never did this before."

Jeremy's eyes widened. "How long a ride would it be to the prison?"

"About three hours at most. An hour of business, whatever that might be, then three hours back, fits the pattern of his new behavior perfectly."

David chewed his cheek for a moment. "But what business could he possibly have?"

Marcus shook his head. "From everything I've seen in this town, I believe we have a mini-tyrant here, and you did say that Simon was being tortured. I wouldn't be surprised if he was the one doing the torturing, or was at least observing it."

Jeremy shook his head. "The bastard! But how? Wouldn't there be questions asked? I mean, Simon was arrested for murder. Shouldn't he have been executed by now?"

Marcus nodded. "Exactly. So the fact he hasn't, means there's more going on here. I think Gilles is some sort of barbarian who enjoys seeing people suffer. I think he somehow has connections at the prison that have allowed him to sneak Simon in there, and then punish our good friend for his own twisted pleasure."

"But how can we prove it?"

Jeremy lay on his side, poking at the fire with a stick. "I say we follow him tomorrow and see where he goes."

Marcus agreed. "Who's the smart boy now?"

David laughed. "There's another thing, though. Have you noticed how everyone seems to be a little, I don't know, off, in this town?"

Marcus frowned. "I noticed it too. Everyone seems terrified of something. Almost nobody has wanted to talk to me, and the few that have, have been attacked, including our host. I'm not sure what it is, but I'm pretty sure Gilles and his men have something to do with it." He shook his head. "Can you believe a town like this has a jail?"

David grunted. "I've never heard of such a thing, not in these parts."

Jeremy agreed, jerking a thumb over his shoulder where the bodies lay out in the cold. "And a Delegate that needs men to help him? How bad could crime possibly be here?"

Marcus sighed. "I've seen these people. They are good people, simply trying to survive. But they seem to have lost any joy in their lives."

Mathilde entered the room carrying a large pot. Jeremy and David leaped to their feet to help her, and soon they were all eating, the old lady refusing any of the food, instead sitting in her chair, enjoying watching them partake in her efforts.

"While you eat, I'm going to tell you a little story, since unless you succeed in your mission, I shall be dead regardless."

Marcus regarded her as he swallowed. "Milady?"

She leaned toward him. "I'm going to tell you what is happening here, and why we are all so afraid."

Marcus drew a quick breath, everyone leaning closer to the old lady as she made herself comfortable. "Please, Milady, tell us."

"It all started after Gilles' father died. He was the Bailiff's Delegate before, for quite some time. A good man, from a better family than any around here. They had more than most, which his wife flaunted from time to time, but other than dressing better than others, and filling the collection plate at church a little more than the rest of us, he wasn't guilty of making anyone feel inferior."

"He sounds like an honorable man."

She nodded. "Oh, he was, he definitely was. He was always fair in his dealings with us, and if it weren't for his wife and son, no one would have had any problems with him. His wife never really fit in here, and like I said, she enjoyed flaunting their position. I think she enjoyed being the richest person in a poor town. They'd be little in Paris, but here? A little can go a long way."

"And Gilles?"

"He was a holy terror, that one. Always getting into trouble, always beating up the smaller boys, even some of the girls. I'm ashamed to admit that I, along with many others, had hoped it was him pushed into the river that day, and not the sweet Christian."

Marcus said nothing, subtly raising a finger to make sure no one else did either.

"When his father died, most of us assumed they'd leave, since they weren't from here originally. But instead, the son was granted the position, apparently his mother the one with the connections that had allowed her husband to be given such an important post." She sighed. "She died soon after, and it didn't take long before things went bad."

Marcus shifted slightly. "What happened?"

She frowned, her knuckles turning white as they gripped the arms of her chair. "He started demanding money from the shopkeepers to protect them."

Marcus' eyes shot wide. "I've never heard of such a thing! Not from a man working for the King. Why didn't anyone report him?"

"Most of us refused to pay him at first, dismissing his demands as idle threats. But we were wrong to do so. We have blacksmiths, stables, outfitters, and many more that serve those heading to and from Paris. We rely on this business, and there is more than enough to keep us all busy, enough so that there is work for multiple vendors in some of the trades. But those who refused to pay, soon found their business drying up, and their suppliers refusing to replenish any stock they might need."

"And Gilles was behind this."

"Absolutely."

"But how did he manage this?"

"He hired some men who would intercept travelers outside of town, demand to know their business, and if they planned to do business with one of us not under his 'protection,' his men would either escort them to a competing business, or through to the next town. Those who didn't cooperate were assaulted, which was usually enough to get the message through. Those are the people who now avoid our town, resulting in all of us losing business, as few did business with only one of us."

Jeremy poked at the fire. "Unbelievable!"

Mathilde nodded. "Indeed. When a business would begin to have difficulty, he'd come by, tell them that he could help if they paid his monthly fee, and those that did, suddenly found their customers returning, and their suppliers once again willing to do business with them." She frowned. "Now most of us pay the money. In fact, I don't know anyone who doesn't except the Duboises. He's becoming rich off the backs of hard-working people, and he has to be stopped."

Jeremy turned to Marcus. "I'm sure if the King's Court heard of this, they'd put an end to it."

Marcus grunted. "Perhaps, though not, perhaps, if the message came from me."

Mathilde regarded him. "Why's that?"

David snickered. "The King, umm, doesn't like the master much."

"Why?"

Marcus shook his head. "Too long to explain." He repositioned himself. "What you've said does answer some questions. We now know why Gilles wouldn't want Simon coming back. If the truth were to come out over what happened when he was a child, enough people might decide that justice needed to be delivered for that crime, and it could threaten his entire illicit business he's set up for himself."

The old woman agreed. "They might, at that. A lot of people still remember that day, and are still bitter over Simon getting away with it. If they knew the truth, they might overcome their fear and take action."

Marcus nodded. "Even if they didn't, Gilles might have feared it *could* happen, so he immediately took action when he heard Simon had returned. He killed your nephew, or had someone do it for him, then arrested Simon for the murder, and claimed he died in a fire, leaving the body there for all to see as a lesson to others, and to show he had delivered justice after thirty years. Instead, he secretly sends Simon to prison in Paris."

David shook his head. "But why? Why not just kill him? He's the Bailiff's Delegate. He could have said Simon tried to escape and it was unavoidable. Nobody would have asked any questions."

Jeremy grunted. "Especially in this town."

Mathilde agreed. "Nobody would dare ask any questions."

Marcus frowned. "The message from Thomas was that Simon wasn't in a good way, and that he was being tortured. Perhaps Gilles wants him tortured for some reason, and he travels to Paris regularly to witness it."

Mathilde leaned forward. "I did say he was a holy terror, and I meant it. That one, when he was a boy, tortured the farm animals, chased the livestock, beat them, killed some. When the farmers complained, he stopped, for the most part, after his father finally put his foot down. But then he took to beating the smaller children. And now? Now he's just as bad. That damned cane of his. He doesn't need it, you know, he just likes to always have it with him, so he can crack anyone he wants on the head when the mood strikes him. He's vicious, I tell you, and it wouldn't surprise me one bit if he was having your poor Simon tortured just for fun."

Marcus sighed. "I think we have little choice. He now knows that you have talked, because he tried to have you killed. He'll know the men he sent to kill you are missing, and will have seen our horses outside. My guess is he'll want to eliminate any loose ends to his crimes."

David frowned. "Meaning Simon."

"Exactly. We have to reach the prison before he does, otherwise I fear he'll be delivering a death sentence for our friend."

Outside La Conciergerie Prison
Paris, Kingdom of France

Marcus stood in the shadows of an alleyway across from the grimness that was La Conciergerie Prison. It was an impressive and depressing structure, and few who entered it involuntarily, ever made their way out. If Simon were indeed housed within these walls these past many weeks, the chances of rescuing him were slim to none.

Yet he had to try.

This was his best friend. Their bond was stronger than that between most brothers, and despite their difference in station, he would happily lay down his life if it meant saving Simon's.

And if he were to lose him to this place, he didn't know how he'd go on. The change in his life, the upheaval in all their lives, had already been tremendous. But for Simon not to be a part of it was unfathomable.

Yet he had sent his friend off to make his own decision on whether to stay, and even should they succeed in freeing him, he still had a decision to make, a decision that could still mean losing him.

His chest ached at the thought, and he shoved the wave of self-pity that threatened to overwhelm him deep down, instead focusing on the task at hand. They had left at the crack of dawn, though not before secreting Mathilde over to Simon's parents' house. They had been shocked to see him, even more so at his request, but they had acquiesced to having the old lady stay with them until he and the others returned.

He left Mathilde to fill them in on the details of their journey, and the possible truth about their son.

He hoped it thawed the old man's heart.

Their early departure had allowed them to beat Gilles to Paris, and he smiled slightly as the man rode up to a side gate of the prison. He had bet that Gilles wouldn't use the main gate, as it might draw attention, whatever he was up to likely requiring discretion.

And the fact he was here so much earlier than normal, confirmed Marcus' fears that he was indeed here to tie up the loose end that was Simon.

His heart hammered at the thought, and he peered down the road, still seeing no sign of the help he had sent David and Jeremy to beg for.

What appeared to be a purse, heavy with coin, was handed over to one of the guards as words were exchanged, and Marcus cursed.

I need to hear them.

He crossed the road as casually as he could, a plain brown surcoat wrapped around him hiding his armor and markings, its hood pulled over his head to hide his face. As he neared, he caught bits and pieces of the conversation, then suddenly heard everything. He stopped and turned, staring down the road, as if waiting for someone, while he cocked an ear to continue his eavesdropping, one eye on the proceedings.

"Getting your fun a little early today, I see."

Gilles shook his head. "No, I'm afraid that today your guest's suffering is over."

"The boys will be disappointed to hear that. Why?"

"Questions are being asked. It's too risky to keep him alive. Besides, we've all had our fun. He wasn't the first, and he won't be the last, though this one was particularly satisfying."

"The boys definitely enjoyed him. He has spirit. It took a long time for him to break."

Gilles nodded. "They all break in the end, though he lasted the longest. I fear I'll never find another like him."

"It's not every day you can work over a Templar."

Rage flared in Marcus' heart at the mention of his Order, all but confirming they were indeed speaking of Simon.

And the fact he was still alive.

"All right, it's clear." The guard opened the small gate and Gilles disappeared inside.

Giving Simon perhaps only moments to live.

Inside La Conciergerie Prison
Paris, Kingdom of France

Simon rushed toward the door as the small opening slid open, a sliver of light marking the arrival of his food. A plate was slid through then a cup of water, but he didn't dare say anything until two extra rolls appeared.

It was her.

"Why don't you ever feed the man in the cell next to me?"

"What man?"

Simon dropped to his stomach and pressed his face against the opening, looking up at the woman. He pointed toward the cell. "That one, where Antoine is. He's starving to death. He needs to be fed."

She shook her head. "I'm sorry, Simon, but there's nobody in that cell. There hasn't been for weeks. In fact, there's no one else in this block, it's only you."

Simon's eyes narrowed. "But that's impossible. I've been speaking to him for days. I've been sharing my food with him. I know he's there."

"I don't know what to say. All the doors are open except yours. Believe me, you're alone here."

"But I've felt his touch! His wife's name is Cateline, his son is Christian! He's a woodcarver from Chartres that works in Paris. Please, you must be mistaken."

But the fear in her eyes told him that she wasn't, at least in her mind. "I-I have to go." She reached down and snapped the opening shut, leaving him once again in the dark, his weakened heart thumping as he tried to comprehend what was just said.

"No!" he cried as his head throbbed again. He steadied his breathing, focusing on the rhythm, latching once again onto the image of Marcus laughing, Jeremy covered in dung, and David nearly crying from laughing so hard.

His head settled, and he gathered his daily offerings, returning to the corner, processing what she had said.

All the doors are open except yours.

In the few times he had peered through the opening, he had noticed other cell doors across the way that were open, yet he was sure he had heard others wailing in agony.

Yet none of that was important.

He had spoken to Antoine for days. He had shared his food with him. He had touched his hand, felt the warmth of his skin.

He took one of the rolls and positioned himself near the hole, his heart beating so hard he could hear it pulse through his ears, and it left him terrified to open his mouth, to ask the question he so desperately had to.

He closed his eyes.

"Antoine, are you there?"

"Well, I was thinking of going for a stroll along the Seine, but I thought I'd hold off until after dinner."

Simon smiled, a sigh of relief escaping. Had she just been playing with him? That had to be it. But why would she do such a thing? Perhaps the guards discovered he was talking with Antoine, and decided to have some fun with him, and forced the poor girl to lie.

He pushed a roll through the hole and Antoine took it.

"You know, the girl who brings the food said you weren't there."

"What are you talking about?"

"She said that your cell is empty, the door is open, and that I've apparently been talking to no one these past days."

Antoine laughed. "Well, I can assure you my cell door is quite closed, that I am sitting here speaking to the only friend I have left in the world, and that your imagination is getting the better of you."

Simon tensed. "My imagination? What do you mean?"

Antoine chuckled. "My friend, I think they must have hit you on the head. What girl are you talking about? Tell me about her! Is she beautiful? Young? Old? Blonde like my wife?"

Simon wasn't sure what to say. Antoine wasn't getting fed, so would never have had occasion to actually see her, but there was no way he hadn't heard their conversations, or his talking of how she was the one responsible for the extra food. "Are you joking with me, Antoine?"

Antoine's voice became serious. "No, my friend, I'm not. I'm concerned. You've been having these bad headaches. Maybe you *were* hit on the head."

"So you honestly don't know of the girl I've been telling you about, the girl who brings us our food?"

"The girl who brings the food? Simon, I'm the one who's been sharing my food with you. The guards bring me my meal each day, they never give you anything, and I give you my roll."

Simon grabbed at his head, the throbbing returning. "But that makes no sense. I have a plate here, I have a cup. She gives me a new one each day."

"My friend, those were always there. We made a game of it, where you'd pretend you were eating a hearty meal each time I handed you my bread. It was always good fun."

Simon seized on something Antoine said. "But I give *you* the roll. Your hand doesn't fit through the hole."

He heard some shuffling then suddenly a hand touched him.

He yelped.

"Wait a moment! I thought your hand didn't fit!"

"It's always fit, my friend. It was yours that didn't."

Simon shook his head, the pounding once again threatening to overwhelm him. "This makes no sense." He dipped his finger in the gruel that was his meal. "But I have the plate of food right here."

"It's all in your head, Simon. We've been playing at that for days."

"But the girl! She was supposed to get word to Marcus, to let him know where I was, to let him know I hadn't betrayed my oath to him!"

"I'm afraid that was all in your head, my friend. There is no girl."

Simon's jaw dropped as he tried to remember everything over the past few days. The conversations, the feedings, the torture, the headaches. It made no sense.

Unless he was going crazy.

And the prospect terrified him, for it was the only explanation. If the girl was real, and telling him the truth, then Antoine wasn't real. And if Antoine was real, and telling him the truth, then the girl wasn't. Either way, he was imagining one of them.

Or perhaps both?

If Antoine was telling the truth, then the hope that had kept him going these past days was false. Nobody had been told of his plight, no friend on the outside was getting word to Marcus, and Marcus would never know that he had died here, desperate to return and fulfill his oath. His friend of over two decades would live the rest of his life thinking he had been betrayed.

Simon rolled onto his side, his shoulders heaving as he sobbed, each jarring motion agony, weakening him even further.

But he didn't care.

Not anymore.

He just wanted to die, to end the pain, to end the suffering. If he was truly losing his mind, he didn't want any part of this existence.

Please, Lord, take me now. Take me while I'm still a man, and not some pathetic madman, screaming in the dark.

But what if the girl was the one telling the truth?

What if she was real, and Antoine wasn't?

He had the food, he was sure of it. Antoine's claims that it was just a game they played, imagining a good meal, sounded completely unfamiliar to him. And if she were telling the truth, that he was alone down here, then Antoine wasn't real.

It still meant he was going insane, imagining a

cellmate, though it meant that there was still hope.

He cried out in rage and frustration.

"What is the truth!"

"The truth, my friend, is that no one is coming for you, and that your master will live on, thinking you betrayed him for the rest of his life."

"No! That isn't true! It can't be!"

Surely, the Lord wouldn't let it end this way. Not after decades of devotion, decades of service in His name. He had killed scores of infidels protecting the Holy Land so those who believed in the Lord could safely make their pilgrimages, and he refused to believe it would all end like this, rotting in a prison cell, slowly going insane, while his master wondered what had happened to him.

"You're going to burn in Hell for all those infidels you killed. Did you really think God wanted you killing in His name?"

Simon rolled into a ball, rocking back and forth as he continued to sob. "Please, stop! Please just leave me alone, let me die."

"As you wish, Simon Chastain."

He heard Antoine's cell door open, causing him even more confusion.

I thought she said the door was open?

"Goodbye, my friend. I hope you enjoy dying alone."

The door slammed shut, Antoine's laugh slowly fading, as a realization settled in.

He *was* real, but he was working for Gilles as he had suspected before.

He felt a flood of renewed hope, then gasped.

If he was real, and was in the next cell, then the girl was lying.

And that meant she could have been lying about everything.

Simon hugged his knees as all hope faded, his heart slowing as his final prayer was granted.

Thank you, my Lord.

Outside La Conciergerie Prison
Paris, Kingdom of France

Marcus stared down the street yet again, and yet again was disappointed. If help were coming, it should have been here by now, but he was foolish to expect any. The Order couldn't risk antagonizing the King any further, and a confrontation at his main prison could provoke the man into taking action, action that the Order might not survive.

Yet he couldn't wait any longer.

Gilles Laurent had been inside for at least several moments, and depending on how swiftly his instructions were carried out, Simon could already be dead, or about to be.

The very thought of his friend dying while he stood outside, doing nothing, tore him apart.

He had no choice.

He had to act alone.

He spun on his heel, rapidly approaching the side gate, tight against the wall so the guard couldn't see his approach, and drew his dagger. He reached the gate, made of iron bars, with ample openings where he could stick a blade through.

"Excuse me, guard!"

The guard Gilles had been speaking to earlier approached. "What do you want? Be off with you!"

Marcus reached through and grabbed the man by the coat, yanking him closer and pressing the tip of his blade against the man's stomach. "I understand you

209

have a friend of mine inside."

The guard stared down at the blade, his eyes wide. "Are you mad? What do you think you're doing?"

With his knife hand, Marcus moved aside the cloak covering his armor and markings, revealing his surcoat with its bright red cross on a field of white. "What is your answer now?"

The guard started to tremble, his face paling. "P-perhaps."

"You're going to take me to him, or die. It's your choice."

The guard drew a deep breath, restoring some of his courage. "You're already dead, you fool. Even if you kill me, the others will still kill you."

The sound of dozens of horses approaching had Marcus' heart leaping, and a smile spreading. He glanced down the street, but still saw nothing. He assumed it was David and Jeremy finally arriving with reinforcements, though he couldn't risk that it might not be.

"My friends are coming. Either you take me to the prisoner you are holding for Gilles Laurent, or I kill you where you stand, then my friends and I storm this prison and free our brother."

The guard's eyes widened with fear as he pressed his face against the bars separating them, trying to see down the road.

His jaw dropped.

Marcus' head spun toward the end of the street, and both pride and relief surged through him as the head of a large column of Templar Knights and sergeants approached, with David and Jeremy flanking the commander leading his brothers in arms. He grabbed the guard by the chin, forcing him to meet his gaze. "Take me to him now, or you'll be the first to die of many."

The guard trembled out a nod, fishing a key from his pocket and unlocking the gate. Marcus stepped inside and closed the gate behind him. The guard reached to lock it when Marcus stopped him.

"We'll leave that unlocked, just in case my friends decide they need to get in here for some reason."

"Fine."

Marcus sensed a hint of courage returning to the man's voice, and quickly dissuaded it with a press of his dagger, hidden under his cloak, into the man's back. "Warn your friends, and you die. This I promise you."

The guard waved at another as they crossed the courtyard toward the ominous structure that housed Simon and so many others, many of whom were probably as innocent as his poor sergeant.

"A visitor who carries a heavy purse. I'll share it with you later."

The other man grinned and turned his back on the proceedings so he could deny he saw anything if questioned later.

Their own corruption would be their undoing this day.

"That's good," whispered Marcus. "Just keep going, calm and steady."

They reached a side door and the guard knocked three times. "It's Gaspard. Let me in."

Marcus heard the door unlock then stepped back as it swung outward. Gaspard stepped inside, jerking a thumb over his shoulder at Marcus.

"A visitor with some coin for us all." Gaspard held out his hand and a set of keys was tossed to him by a bored guard, excitement evidently not something in abundance here.

Marcus said nothing, instead following Gaspard down a set of stairs to another door. He kept track of their journey deep into the dungeon, but soon realized there was no getting back out without help.

And that troubled him immensely.

They finally reached an outer chamber with two guards. Gaspard greeted them with a wave. "Is our friend still here?"

One of the guards shook his head. "No, he just left."

"And our Templar?"

"I was just about to collect him. Can you believe that after all this time of keeping him alive, he wants him racked? What a way to go!"

Gaspard agreed. "I need to see him."

"Sure." The guard rose to unlock the door, then finally noticed Marcus. "Who's this?"

"Just someone who wants to see him before he dies."

The guard paused for a moment.

"Someone with a heavy purse."

The guard grinned. "My favorite kind!"

The door was unlocked and swung open, revealing a set of cells inside, all the doors open save one.

"Where is he?" asked Gaspard.

The guard pointed at the only closed door. "In that one."

"The key?"

212

The guard held it up and Gaspard took it.

Marcus drew his sword and swung, decapitating the first guard, then disemboweling his partner. It took only moments. Gaspard's jaw slackened, then the keys hit the floor as he turned even paler in the torchlight.

"Wh-why did you do that?"

"Two less to fight on the way out, and punishment for what they did to my sergeant and a member of the Order." He pointed at the keys on the floor. "Pick them up."

Gaspard bent over and retrieved the keys with shaking hands. Marcus shoved him inside the cellblock and pointed at the closed door. "Open it."

Gaspard took a moment to get the key in the hole, but finally managed, and swung the door open. Marcus grabbed a torch off the wall and shoved Gaspard inside the cell lest he try anything, then followed. He waved the torch in front of him, peering into the darkness as he struggled to ignore the stench.

Then he spotted an emaciated figure huddled in a corner, trembling with fear. Marcus stepped closer, and the man finally turned his head to look at him.

And Marcus' chest tightened and tears filled his eyes at the sight.

"Simon!"

Simon raised a hand, blocking out the torchlight that now filled his cell, giving his eyes a chance to adjust. He recognized the voice, and his heart leaped at the possibility of it being real, but it couldn't be. There was no way his master was here, there was no way his friend could be inside the prison.

213

He was a figment of his imagination, just as he still feared Antoine might have been.

In fact, Marcus' presence here now confirmed his worst fears.

He had gone mad.

Days if not weeks ago.

Just as they all did.

No man could withstand the constant torture. It was impossible. Not the kind he had undergone. All would break eventually, or die before they had the chance, if their torturers weren't expert in their technique.

Unfortunately his were, and they had kept him alive all this time, long enough to apparently break his mind.

And if they had, he wondered what he might have said during those sessions that he didn't even realize. Had he told them what they wanted to hear? Had he confessed to the crimes he hadn't committed?

The very idea crushed him, and tears streamed down his cheeks. "Forgive me, Lord, I never meant to!"

"You never meant to what?"

It was the hallucination of his friend once again, an imagined contrivance created by his defeated mind to help him through his final days, a last-ditch effort to maintain his sanity, though its very existence meant he was anything but sane. He moved his hand and could see a concerned Marcus kneeling in front of him, another man he recognized as one of the guards who sometimes tortured him, standing in the far corner, appearing terrified.

Simon squeezed his eyes shut, shaking his head

back and forth. "No! Go away! You're not real! I realize that now! None of you are real!" He sucked in a breath, trying to stifle his sobs. "I'm not insane. I can't be insane. If I know you're not real, then I can't be insane. An insane man would think you're real."

Someone grabbed his hand and Simon flinched, trying to withdraw his emaciated limb, and failing. Marcus held it against his chest.

"I'm here, my friend. Feel the warmth of my skin, the beat of my heart. Hear my voice. You're going to be all right. Our brothers are outside these walls as I speak, awaiting us. If we don't come out in good order, they will assault this prison and come for us." Marcus reached out and gripped Simon's shoulder. "It's over, my friend."

Simon shook his head, tearing his hand away. "I-I don't believe you. You *can't* be here. Everything you say is merely what I want to hear. You're my mind playing tricks on me. Just like with Antoine. He wasn't real, and neither are you."

Marcus smiled gently. "Tell me of Antoine."

Simon stole a glance toward the hole, relieved to see it was actually there, and not a figment of his imagination. This was the first time he had laid eyes on it, the first time light had graced this cell in its full brilliance.

He pointed.

"Through there, on the other side. He-he was my friend. He helped me." Simon sighed. "But he wasn't real. And neither are you."

Marcus rose then stepped outside, returning a moment later. "Did you feed him?"

Simon paused. "I-I thought so, but he said that he

was the one feeding me."

Marcus stepped closer. "But you thought you were feeding him."

"Yes. The girl, the girl that brings the food. She was giving me extra, and I would put it through the hole. But she said that there was no one there, and he said that he was the one feeding me. One of them is lying, but now that I see you here, then I know he wasn't real, because you're not real. I know she was telling the truth, that he was never there."

"Is this the girl you told to get word to me?"

"Yes."

"Her name is Sabine."

Simon's eyes narrowed. "Why do I know that name?"

"She was the girl who Mrs. Thibault had fake an illness, so she could put her own person into the prison. Do you remember?"

Simon gasped as he remembered, and a pit formed in his stomach as he jabbed a finger at Marcus. "See! Again, a name I know! Why do I know all the names? Why was Antoine's wife a name I knew, why was his son the name of the boy I stood accused of killing?" His eyes opened wide. "And he was a woodworker! I imagined his carvings, and they were those that Pierre plays with! Everything Antoine said, everything you are saying now, is taken from my mind! None of it is real!"

Marcus kneeled in front of him once again. "I want you to listen to me, my friend. Sabine is a real person, you know that. And someone brought you food every day, otherwise you'd be long dead. Can we agree on that?"

Simon regarded him for a moment, then nodded. "Y-yes."

"Good. Then if Antoine wasn't real, then Sabine must have been, right?"

"I-I suppose. Though maybe Antoine was real?"

"Yes, that is possible. But let's assume for a moment he wasn't. He was a creation of your own mind."

"As you are."

Marcus chuckled. "You're not going to make this easy, are you?"

Simon smiled, praying that the vision in front of him was actually his friend. "Do I ever?"

"So, if we assume you were being fed, and we assume Antoine wasn't real, then we can safely assume that Sabine was the one giving you food. So if she was, then she was the one you told to get word to me. It was a difficult path to find you, but I did, and when we get you out of here, we'll be bringing Gilles Laurent to justice."

Simon quickly inhaled at the mention of his nemesis' name. "So it *was* him."

"It was. And to prove I am real, and you are not insane, I need you to take my hand, and step through that door. I have something you need to see that I hope will convince you that Sabine was real, and therefore I am here because of the message you gave her."

Simon closed his eyes and said a silent prayer, asking the Lord for guidance.

A warmth spread through him, his shivers from the cold disappearing, and he wasn't certain if it were the Lord's doing, or his own body renewing itself with

217

the energy that hope brings, but it was enough for him to force out a nod.

"Very well."

He held out his hands and Marcus took them, pulling him to his feet. His friend put his arm over his shoulders and helped him through the door, practically carrying him to the next cell, its door open just as Sabine had said.

Marcus pushed the torch through the door. "Tell me, my friend, what do you see?"

Simon shuffled forward, examining the filthy surroundings, then gasped as he spotted the opposite side of the hole that had provided him so much comfort.

And the pile of uneaten rolls that lay in front of it, only the rats having partaken of his painfully sacrificed bounty.

"H-he was never here!"

Marcus nodded. "Exactly. Which means Sabine is real, and she was the one giving you the food. And she's the one who got a message to Thomas Durant, who came to the farm to tell us of your fate." Marcus turned him around to face him. "I'm real, my friend, and if you trust me, I'll have you out of here in no time. I just need you to trust me."

Simon stared in his friend's eyes, still filled with uncertainty, then glanced over his shoulder at the pile of uneaten food, lovingly shared with Antoine.

Then took a leap of faith.

He collapsed into his friend's arms, sobbing without shame, deciding that even if this was a hallucination, it was one worth embracing fully, and in time, the truth would reveal itself.

THE SERGEANT'S SECRET

If it hadn't already.

Outside La Conciergerie Prison
Paris, Kingdom of France

David's heart pounded as he sat on his horse, two score of Templar cavalry, a mix of knights in their bright white, and sergeants in their black, lined up in an impressive show of force in front of the terrifyingly grim prison that lay before them.

He had spotted Marcus entering the moment they rounded the corner, his master evidently fearing there was no time to wait for them, and he had desperately wanted to follow, though the commander of the column held him back.

"We will not be attacking here, today. We are merely out on parade, and happen to be passing here. *That* is our official story, understood?"

David had reluctantly agreed, but had to give Jeremy a look to calm the more impulsive of their group before he said something unwise.

It felt like hours, though was only moments, before he finally saw activity through the small entrance Marcus had used earlier, his position allowing him to see deep into the courtyard. A side door opened, and three men emerged, one carried in another's arms, the arms of his master, Sir Marcus.

And his heart sank, for the man he carried couldn't be Simon, this man half the size of their friend.

He gasped out a cry as they neared and he finally saw his face. Simon was gaunt, emaciated, as pale as the gray of the prison that had housed him, and as near death as any man he had seen.

"Is that him?" asked the commander, his voice barely a whisper, too shocked at the sight.

"I-I fear it is."

"Bring forward a spare horse and a transport!"

"Yes, sir!"

David ignored the goings on, instead dismounting with Jeremy and walking toward the gate. He reached through and tried the handle, and to his surprise, it opened. He swung it out of the way, and they both rushed through toward their friends.

Tears streaked Jeremy's face at the sight. "D-does he live?"

"He does, but barely."

David was at a loss for words, when he heard angry shouts coming from the prison. A man, his uniform suggesting he might be the commandant, was rushing down a large set of steps, half a dozen guards on his heels.

"Halt!"

David drew his bow, readying an arrow, as did Jeremy, and they covered Marcus' exit with Simon in his arms. Through the gates, they fell back through the wall of cavalry as the man and his guards arrived.

"What goes on here?"

Marcus laid Simon in the cart that had been brought forward, and Jeremy immediately gave him water as David joined his master.

"An injustice, that's what!"

The man stared at Marcus. "And who are you to make such a judgment?"

"I am Sir Marcus de Rancourt, and that man I just liberated from your prison is my sergeant, Simon

Chastain."

The man eyed him. "I don't recognize the name, and I know all who are within these walls."

Marcus stepped closer, and the entire column advanced with him. "Then I think you have a problem that may be bigger than just one man." He jabbed a finger at the guard he had come out with. "I suggest you interrogate this man, and ask him of his dealings with Gilles Laurent of Le Chesnay. Apparently, he has been bringing prisoners here to torture, for fun, for quite some time. He has been paying off your guards, and I hope for your sake it is something you were unaware of."

The man's face burned red from anger, and he spun around, rapidly advancing on the guard. "Is what he says true? Have you been taking bribes and torturing innocent men behind *my* walls?"

David was certain the guard had soiled himself. He suppressed a grin at the shocked look, then let a sigh of relief go as the man quickly yielded.

"It is."

The guard was shoved back through the gates, and the commandant turned to address Marcus. "Sir Marcus, I apologize for what has happened here, and for what has happened to your sergeant. You can rest assured that justice will be delivered, and that this will never happen again."

Marcus bowed his head. "Then that is all I can ask."

The man returned the acknowledgment, then disappeared behind the gate that slammed shut a moment later. A horse was brought forward for Marcus and he mounted it, and without saying a word, took off after the cart carrying Simon and Jeremy, the rest of the column turning and following at a more orderly pace.

David followed his master at a gallop, saying a silent prayer for his friend, fearing it might already be too late.

223

Enclos du Temple, Templar Fortress
Paris, Kingdom of France
One week later

Simon sat up in his bed, feeding himself a bowl of soup, feeling almost his old self. The nuns at the Templar headquarters for France had nursed him back to health quite expertly, and his emaciated frame was recovering, albeit slowly.

It would take weeks, if not months, to recover fully from what Gilles Laurent had done to him. He didn't care if it weren't by the man's own hand. Gilles had given the instructions, and had to be stopped from doing it again.

For Simon wasn't the first.

Nor, according to what Marcus had overheard, would have been the last.

And no one else should ever endure what he had.

Part of him was ashamed of what had happened to him. Not the physical side of things. There was no shame in crying out in pain, of begging for mercy, or of wishing to die if it would only end the suffering.

No shame whatsoever.

He had endured for over a month, and hadn't once confessed to crimes he had never committed.

His shame came from his hallucinations, his imaginings. He knew now that everything around him was real, that his friends were here with him, and that his suffering was over, though it had taken several days for him to be sure.

But as his strength returned, so did his mental faculties, and it was the image of the uneaten rolls that he kept coming back to, whenever he wondered if Antoine were indeed real.

"Look who I found."

Marcus entered the room, followed by a young woman, her head bowed, her fingers crossed together at her waist. She curtsied, saying nothing.

Simon stared at her then gasped, twisting his head to see her from the angle he had. "Is it you? My savior?"

She flushed. "I would hardly call myself that."

Simon smiled, holding out his hand for her. She reluctantly approached and took it. "My good woman, if it weren't for you, I would have certainly died in there. I shall thank the Lord for bringing you to me, for the rest of my days."

Tears filled her eyes. "I-I'm just so happy to see you out of there. Nobody should endure what you did."

Simon looked past her at Marcus. "How did you find her?"

Marcus stepped deeper into the room. "I was paying my *respects* to Mrs. Thibault, encouraging her to forgive Master Durant's absence, when she graciously told me how we could find this young woman."

"I'm surprised you didn't have to pay," muttered Sabine.

Marcus chuckled. "She knew not to bother asking a poor soldier of the Order." He stepped closer. "However, when you leave here, you will find that the Order itself is quite grateful, and will be rewarding you handsomely."

Sabine's eyes widened and her mouth opened, no words coming out. Simon smiled at her, squeezing her hand. "I'm pleased for you."

She stared at him then snapped her jaw shut. She kissed his hand, tears streaming down her cheeks. "I-I'm ashamed to say this, but when you asked me for help, my first instinct was to profit from your misery. It was that young man, Thomas, I think his name was, who insisted I help you. He-he deserves any reward, not me. I was merely a greedy fool who tried to take advantage."

Simon drew her closer. "Nonsense. You spoke to me when no one else would. That took courage. Then even if your next actions were misguided, rather than taking the money Thomas gave you and helping yourself, you helped me. You didn't have to do that. Don't punish yourself for being desperate. So many of us are. Take your reward, and enjoy it. Make your life better for you and your family, with my blessing."

She clasped his hand against her chest. "You are a far better man than any I have known."

Simon shook his head, glancing at Marcus. "I've met better."

Marcus flushed, turning away.

"I-I should leave you to recover."

Simon nodded, letting go of her hand. "Thank you, once again."

She curtsied once more, then backed out of the room, as if in the presence of royalty. Marcus motioned to a squire standing in the hallway. "Take her to the commander. He wants to thank her, and give her the reward."

"Yes, sir."

Two nuns entered, going about their business as if he weren't there.

"Do you want me to leave?" asked Marcus as bandages were unwrapped.

Simon shrugged. "You've seen me at my worst. Why bother?"

Marcus laughed. "I have that, my friend." He leaned in closer to examine the wounds, mostly around Simon's wrists and ankles, the beatings apparently designed to limit actual cuts and gashes that might become infected and lead to his early demise. "How is he looking?"

One of the nuns glanced at him then resumed her work. "His recovery is coming along quite nicely. Soon these will be a distant memory."

Simon frowned. "I fear the wounds may disappear, but the memory shall remain fresh for a long time."

Their work done, the nuns left as quickly as they had come, leaving Marcus and Simon alone.

"Any word from David and Jeremy?"

"Yes, they arrived safely and are at your parents' house along with Mathilde, the woman who helped me prove your innocence. When you're feeling up to it, we'll join them and end this charade, once and for all."

Simon frowned. "We have to leave now. It's too dangerous for them until Gilles is brought to justice."

"You're in no condition to travel."

"Nonsense. I feel almost my old self."

"You lie."

"I do, but it's how well I do it that should matter."

Marcus tossed his head back, laughing. "I've

missed you my friend, more than you shall ever know."

"And I you. But that aside, we should leave in the morning. We can be there in half a day."

Marcus stared at him for a moment then sighed. "Very well. If you fall ill and die, I'll have you resurrected so I can kill you myself."

Simon grinned. "Understood."

Marcus sat on the edge of his bed. "Now, let's talk about what happened when you were a child. You didn't push Christian into the river, did you?"

Simon shook his head. "No, no one did."

Marcus regarded him. "What do you mean?"

"Gilles pushed him into an old abandoned well, just outside of the town."

Marcus' eyes widened. "And they never found the body." He smiled slightly. "Then that means the body is still in that well."

Simon's head slowly bobbed. "Yes, I suppose so."

Marcus leaned closer, excited. "Tell me exactly what happened. Don't leave out a single detail."

Chastain Residence
Le Chesnay, Kingdom of France

Simon's mother gasped then rushed toward him, wrapping her arms around his now slight frame. "What did they do to you?"

His father kept a distance, much to Marcus' disappointment, the man evidently not yet willing to believe his son was innocent. Marcus turned to David and Jeremy as the reunion continued.

"Any problems?"

"There have been men on horseback riding by on a regular basis, always stopping and making a point to be seen. They've been getting bolder as each day passed." David frowned. "I fear if you hadn't arrived when you did, things might have taken a turn for the worse." He patted Tanya. "I think half the reason they kept away is because of her."

Marcus smiled at Tanya, and she stared up at him, her tail wagging, clearly excited to see him. He gave her a scratch. "She's definitely proven handy, hasn't she?"

Marcus regarded Simon as he fell into a nearby chair. His poor friend was exhausted, the journey long even for a healthy man, but he had said nothing to complain the entire way, even when they had gone around the town so no one would see the resurrected Simon's return. Marcus had made a point of frequently stopping, insisting his friend eat and drink at every possible occasion.

And now he wondered if they should wait for him

229

to regain his strength, or finish what needed finishing.

Now.

Unfortunately, the decision appeared to have been made for him, if David's concerns weren't to be ignored. Gilles would probably make his move tonight once he received word of new arrivals. And that move, he feared, would be to burn them out, rather than take them head-on. Though they might all survive such an occurrence, it would leave the Chastains without a home. And with a town as terrified as this one, neighbors would not be there to help them rebuild as they might in any other.

As they had in Crécy-la-Chapelle.

Marcus stepped over to Simon. "How do you feel?"

Simon was about to rise when Marcus held out a hand. "You don't look well."

He grunted. "Nor do I feel it. But what must be done must be done now, before it is too late."

"Let me get a hot meal in him first," said Mrs. Chastain. "It's already prepared. Eat that, warm yourself by the fire, and you can leave in good order, to do whatever it is you must do."

Marcus nodded. "An excellent idea, Mrs. Chastain."

Mathilde appeared with a tisane, handing it to Simon. "Here, this will help warm those bones."

Simon smiled gratefully, quickly partaking, his food soon delivered by his mother.

"And just what is it you propose to do now that you are here?"

Marcus turned to Mr. Chastain. "Reveal the truth

230

about what happened here a month ago, and thirty years ago."

Mr. Chastain stared at his son for a moment, then returned his gaze to Marcus. "And you know?"

"Yes, I do."

"And you can prove it?"

"I think I can."

Mr. Chastain stepped forward. "Then I would like to come with you."

Mrs. Chastain stood by her husband. "I as well."

Marcus bowed slightly. "I'm afraid with things the way they are, you will *all* have to come with us. I can't risk leaving you alone here, unguarded."

David cleared his throat. "Then you have something for us to do?"

"Perhaps the most important thing of all."

Jeremy sighed. "This is what happens when you're so good at what you do. The toughest assignments always become yours."

David snorted. "I think it's because *I'm* so good at *my* job, and you just happen to always be underfoot when glory comes my way."

Marcus chuckled. "You may not be so pleased once I tell you what I require of you."

Town Center
Le Chesnay, Kingdom of France

David rode at a trot through the town, Jeremy at his side, his heart racing with the foolishness of what they were doing. They wore their brown surcoats with red cross, signifying their position within the Order, and drew the attention of every single person they passed.

Exactly Marcus' intention.

They reached the other end of the town and came to a halt, turning their beasts around.

David looked at Jeremy. "Are you ready?"

"Yes. But let's hurry, for I fear I want to keep heading for Paris."

David chuckled. "Then let's get this over with."

"May I make a suggestion first?"

"What's that?"

"I suggest we both stop doing our jobs so well, so we can avoid such assignments in the future."

David tossed his head back, laughing. "A fantastic idea, but I think all that will be necessary is for me to lower myself to your level." He urged his horse forward before Jeremy could reply, a grin on his face. He took the right side of the road, Jeremy the left, and as he approached the first set of shops, he sat high in his saddle, drawing in a breath of courage, then as loud as he could, delivered the message he had been instructed to give.

"If you want to know the truth about Simon Chastain, and what happened to Roland and Christian, then gather at Roland's home right now!"

Jeremy repeated the message on the other side, and within moments, it passed faster than he could ride. He repeated it, verbatim, as he continued through the town, and back toward the Chastain residence. He glanced behind him to see ever-increasing numbers of the residents leaving their shops and the booths set up out front of them, eagerly talking among themselves, and smiled.

Jeremy rode up beside him. "I think our work here is done."

David nodded. "And now for our most important task."

Roland Villeneuve Residence
Le Chesnay, Kingdom of France

Marcus stood on the small porch that led to the late Roland Villeneuve's home, his white Templar surcoat proudly displayed, his shoulders drawn back and his chin held high, striking as strong an authoritative figure as he could without it being comical.

It had the desired effect.

The town was gathering rapidly, David and Jeremy clearly having succeeded in their first mission, and he hoped would do as well in their second, more critical one. For if they failed, all about to happen would be a waste, and his sergeant could still hang.

"Look."

Marcus glanced at Mathilde, standing behind him with Simon's parents, then followed her gaze to see Gilles and half a dozen of his men riding up, a shiver of fear rushing through the gathered crowd.

Exactly as Marcus had hoped.

It will be your overconfidence that will be your undoing.

"And just what is going on here?"

Marcus bowed his head at the new arrivals. "We're going to learn the truth of what happened here one month ago, and what happened thirty years ago."

The mention of the childhood incident rattled Gilles, and he stared blankly at Marcus for a moment. "Break this up! Everyone go back home!"

Marcus stepped forward, flicking his surcoat aside to reveal his sword, the crowd that had begun to turn,

234

pausing to see what might happen next. "Do you fear the truth?"

Gilles glared at him. "Of course not!"

Marcus smiled, waving a hand at the gathered townsfolk. "Then why send these people away? Why not let them hear the truth?"

"Your *version* of the truth, but not the truth."

"If you are so confident in *your* version, then you shouldn't fear a challenge to it."

"Let him speak!" shouted someone from the back, and murmurs of agreement rippled through the people, followed by a few courageous shouts.

The crowd was on his side.

And it was essential that they be, for if they weren't, the likelihood of them believing anything he said was probably nil.

Marcus smiled at Gilles. "I think your people have spoken."

Gilles turned red and his nostrils flared, his hand gripping his trademark cane squeezing so hard, his knuckles went white.

Then he exhaled loudly, the red turning pink.

He smiled.

"Very well. I'll allow this little bit of entertainment, for that is all it is. A fiction created by a man who knows nothing of us, or the suffering we have been through, all caused by his sergeant, Simon Chastain, who we all know was a murderer, both as a child, and a man."

Too many heads bobbed in the crowd for Marcus' liking, but he was here to undo thirty years of steadfast belief, and had barely spoken a word.

Gilles seemed emboldened and dismounted. "Let this cretin spout his nonsense. It changes nothing! Simon Chastain murdered Roland when he arrived here a month ago, just as he murdered poor Christian before my eyes when we were children. Nothing you say here can change that, and as Simon has already paid for his crimes with his own life, I fail to see the benefit. But please, present us your fiction."

Marcus bowed graciously with a smile. "I thank you for the time." He straightened and met Gilles' gaze, the smile wiped from his face. "And yes, Simon has paid for his crimes, more dearly than any man should have, I'm sure."

Gilles' eyes narrowed. "What do you mean?"

"I think you've done enough talking." Marcus turned to face the crowd, many with shocked expressions at the slight just delivered, then paused, returning his attention to Gilles. "I'm sorry, but would you like to get closer? It appears you're having a hard time seeing past all these people."

Gilles flushed at the subtle insult concerning his height as several in the crowd snorted. He was by no means a short man, though he wasn't tall either. Simply of average height and slight in features. He glared at Marcus. "You dare insult me, sir?"

Marcus held up his hands. "I'm sorry, I wasn't aware that being of your stature was considered a shortcoming. Some of the greatest warriors I have ever known aren't, shall we say, of my height. In the saddle, all men are equal." He held out his hand, urging the crowd to part. "Please, make room for our Bailiff's Delegate."

The crowd parted, a red-faced Gilles forced to

236

advance, otherwise risk additional ridicule.

Marcus nodded at the trademark cane. "That's an interesting cane you have. Do you have an ailment that requires it?"

Gilles shook his head as he mounted the porch. "No, it was my father's. I carry it to honor him."

Marcus bowed his head. "I hear he was an honorable man."

"He was."

"Now that you are here, let us resume." Marcus turned back to the crowd. "These good people are gathered to hear what I have to say. Many of you were alive when Christian Samuel died thirty years ago, and you've heard the story told by Gilles Laurent and backed up by Roland Villeneuve. You remember that Gilles said Simon got into a fight with Christian, and in a fit of anger, shoved him into the river, where he fell through the ice and drowned, his body never found. You also have heard how Gilles heroically fought with Simon, to try and prevent him from escaping, and in that fight, how his prized Parisian shirt was torn."

Heads were bobbing among those of age as they all recalled the events, and for those too young, they reassured them that what had just been said was true.

Marcus smiled. "I see everyone agrees with what I have just said?"

Universal nods.

He turned to Gilles. "Do you have anything to add?"

Gilles' shook his head, appearing calmer as his version of events had just been relayed. "Keep going. You're just reconfirming what we all have known most of our lives."

Marcus beamed. "Thank you for confirming everything I just said as your version." He turned back to the crowd, though not before noticing with satisfaction Gilles' startled expression as he scrambled to interpret Marcus' words. "Now to more recent events. A month ago, Simon returned, and that same night, Roland was found murdered in his home." He gestured toward the house behind him. "*This* home." He turned to Gilles. "Please, sir, tell us how he died."

Gilles seemed caught off guard, but quickly recovered. "As the King's representative, I'd be happy to. It is my expert opinion that Roland was killed by a blade, most likely a sword, thrust through his stomach then twisted. Roland would have bled out quite quickly."

"So he bled out on the floor."

"Yes."

"And was he alive when your witness found him?"

Gilles shook his head. "No, he was dead already."

"And how long had he been dead?"

Gilles shrugged. "Not long. The body was still warm."

"And how did you know Simon had done it?"

"One of my men saw him leaving in a hurry. Simon's haste had my man concerned."

"And can we speak to this man?"

Gilles frowned. "Unfortunately, he was killed recently."

Marcus pursed his lips, meeting Gilles' stare, knowing full well his opponent was aware by whose hand the man had likely died. "That's unfortunate."

"Indeed."

"Yes, it is unfortunate that the only witness to Simon's alleged crime was not only one of your men, but now cannot be questioned." Gilles opened his mouth to protest when Marcus cut him off. "Fortunately, I'm sure he told you everything he knew, and we can rely on your excellent recollection of that night, can we not?"

Gilles glared at him. "Of course."

"Then please, tell us, did your man go inside?"

"He only opened the door."

"He didn't go inside to make sure Roland wasn't still alive?"

"No, it was plain to him from the amount of blood on the floor that he was dead."

"He didn't call out to him?"

"I'm sure he did."

Marcus eyed him. "You're *sure?*"

Gilles flushed. "He never mentioned it, though I'm sure he would have."

Marcus batted a hand. "It's of no importance. Your man said Roland was dead. I assume he then found you, and you returned to confirm the death?"

"Yes."

"And how long did that take?"

"I'm not sure. Less than an hour."

"Did you enter and confirm the death?"

"I most certainly did."

"And how did you confirm this?"

"I felt his neck and chest. I held my hand over his mouth. It was evident he wasn't breathing, that his heart no longer beat, and that most of his blood was on the floor."

"That must have been a horrible sight."

Gilles nodded. "It was. I've known Roland all of my life. I considered him a friend."

Several snickers suggested some in the crowd thought otherwise.

"Now, with so much blood, how did you manage to check on Roland's condition without getting yourself covered in blood?"

Gilles smiled at him. "I'm not a fool. I simply went around the pool of blood, and checked him from behind, where there was little."

Marcus bowed his head. "Of course, of course. After all, you are an expert in these matters."

Gilles shrugged. "Murders seem to only occur here when your sergeant is about."

Gilles' men laughed, several of the townsfolk joining in before they were silenced with glares from their neighbors. It was clear the crowd wasn't on their oppressor's side, and even appeared slightly emboldened.

Marcus cut off all the laughter. "It was a fortunate coincidence your man just happened to be all the way out here, at the exact right moment to see Simon flee the scene."

Gilles glared at him. "What are you suggesting?"

Marcus shrugged. "I'm suggesting nothing." He gestured toward the cane. "May I see it? It is very impressive."

Gilles eyed him for a moment, likely trying to figure out what Marcus' game was, then finally handed it over.

Marcus examined it. It was well worn, though of fine craftsmanship, with a carved top in the form of a sprouting fleur-de-lis, and a copper tipped bottom, flattened from years of use. He tossed it up and grabbed it by the shaft. "Now, there is something I need to show you inside. There isn't much room. In preparation, I've had lanterns and torches lit, and all the windows opened so you can gather around and look through, but please, people, let's realize that not everyone will get to see what I'm about to show, so relay what you see to those behind you."

He stepped inside, placing the cane against the wall as Gilles followed along with Mathilde and Simon's parents, and half a dozen of the crowd, before Marcus held up a hand, cutting them off. The windows quickly filled with faces pressed into the narrow openings, Roland never able to afford to outfit them with glass.

Gilles was red again, his eyes like daggers as he probably suspected something was about to be revealed that would challenge his version of events. "You are trying my patience, Templar. If you don't finish this soon, I will."

Marcus smiled. "Oh, this won't take long at all." He pointed at the large bloodstain, several candles and lanterns placed strategically so it would be plain for all to see. "This is where you found the body."

"Obviously."

"And he was dead."

"Yes."

Marcus used his finger to indicate generally the size of the stain. "As you can see, there was so much blood, he clearly bled to death."

Gilles growled. "Clearly."

Marcus pointed to the two footprints he had discovered earlier. "Note these footprints."

Gilles flushed slightly. "Yes. What of them?"

"Well, what do you make of them?"

Gilles shrugged. "What should I make of them?"

"Well, do you notice how they are clearly visible? There's no blood, just voids in the blood, as if someone stood while Roland bled out."

Gilles snorted. "Of course. Simon stood and watched him die. What's so strange about that?"

"Then you would agree that if these footprints were made after the fact, for example, if *you* had come into the room and discovered the body, and accidentally stepped in the pool of blood, then there would be blood *inside* these footprints, not bare wood as we're seeing."

Gilles paused, as if searching for words, his ears now matching his cheeks in their shade of red. He finally replied, his voice slightly lower than normal. "Yes."

Marcus smiled, responding boisterously. "Of course you would! You're an intelligent man!" He looked at the faces surrounding him. "Does everyone agree, that if the blood had already been there, and someone stepped in that blood, that the footprints would still be evident, but the floor would still be covered in blood?"

All those in the room, and visible through the windows, bobbed their heads, and he could hear the revelations being relayed beyond the walls, those outside shouting their agreement.

"Excellent!" He turned to Gilles. "Now, good sir,

would you do me a favor?"

Gilles didn't appear at all willing. "What?"

"Stand in the footprints."

The crowd gasped and Gilles' eyes shot wide. "Whatever for?"

"For curiosity's sake, please."

For the first time, Gilles appeared genuinely rattled, and his red cheeks paled as he took a step back. "I'll do no such thing."

Marcus drew his dagger and stepped forward, pressing the tip under Gilles' chin, sending those gathered into shock. "I'm afraid I must insist." He grabbed him by the shirt and dragged him toward the stain with ease, Gilles no match for Marcus' size or strength.

Gilles' shoulders slumped as an audible sigh escaped, the will to fight gone from the man. He stepped into the prints, gasps filling the room.

Marcus stared down to make certain what he had suspected had just been proven. And smiled. "Interesting. They seem to match exactly." Gilles tried to step back but Marcus gripped the back of the man's neck, holding him in place. "I think it is quite evident that a man with feet *exactly* the same size as yours, stood here, watching poor Roland bleed out, wouldn't you agree?"

Murmurs of assent filled the small home, but Gilles remained silent, instead staring down at his feet.

Marcus stared at him. "Well?"

Gilles tore his eyes away, glancing at Marcus for a moment, before staring at the void that would have been Roland's body. "No, I wouldn't."

243

"You wouldn't?"

"I mean, yes, I would, but it doesn't mean it was me."

Marcus eyed him for a moment then let him go, Gilles quickly stepping back. "No, I suppose not. I suppose it is possible that a man with the exact same sized feet as you could have committed the murder." He held up a finger. "And while we're on the subject of the size of men's feet, I can assure you that my sergeant's feet were much larger than this."

Gilles seized on the statement as he struggled to regain the upper hand. "And are we to take your word for it? How can we possibly know?"

Marcus pursed his lips, his head slowly bobbing. "You're right. You said he died in the fire."

"He did!"

Marcus sighed. "Then perhaps we'll never know." He stepped back then stopped. "Oh, wait! I almost forgot! There's one *small* matter remaining. A *very* small matter, in fact." He pointed at the floor, to the right of the footprints. "Do you see that little mark in the blood? Another void? As if something very small was in the way of the blood as it flowed from our dearly departed friend?"

Those inside leaned closer, and when spotted, quickly went to the windows to relay what they had seen.

Marcus turned to Gilles. "What do you think it is?"

Gilles shook his head. "I haven't the foggiest idea."

Marcus stepped over to the wall and retrieved Gilles' cane. "Let's try something, shall we?"

Gilles' eyes widened with each step Marcus took toward the bloodstain. He backed away and Marcus grabbed him by the tunic once again, hauling him back into position. He carefully placed the flattened tip of the cane into the tiny void and smiled.

"Well, what do you know? It fits perfectly." He pressed the cane into Gilles' hand. "And look how natural it looks with you standing there, in those perfectly sized footprints, holding your cane, its tip in that tiny void." Marcus put his hand on the hilt of his sword. "Would you have us believe that one of your men just happened to be passing by this property when Simon Chastain fled, after murdering someone he hadn't seen in thirty years? Would you have us believe that Simon's feet happened to be the exact same size as yours, and that he also carried a cane, just like yours?"

It wasn't rage in Gilles' eyes anymore, it was fear.

Yet it lasted only a moment.

He stepped away from the stain, gripping his cane by the shaft, holding the handle up as if it were a weapon. "You have no proof!"

Marcus shrugged. "No, I don't. It's unfortunate that my sergeant isn't here to show that his feet are considerably larger than yours."

"But I am here, Sir Marcus."

Marcus smiled and turned to face the door where a figure stood, his features covered in a dark robe. Simon removed it with a flourish, and gasps were joined by several screams and what Marcus was certain were the sounds of several people hitting the ground outside, overcome with the surprise.

Gilles' eyes were wide, his mouth agape. "But you're supposed to be dead!"

The much larger Simon approached him.

"Fortunately, you are mistaken."

"But I—" Gilles clamped his mouth shut as his eyes roamed the room, searching for some means of escape.

Marcus leaned closer. "What was that you were about to say? That you gave orders at La Conciergerie Prison to have him killed a week ago?"

Gilles backed away. "I, um, no, I did no such thing!"

Marcus scratched his chin. "Interesting. I have several witnesses who claim you did. In fact, the guard you've been bribing, Gaspard, has already sworn out a statement to a representative from the King's Court that you have been paying them for years to hold prisoners there, while you participated in their torture." Marcus grabbed him by the throat, lifting him off the floor. "Do you deny it?"

"I-I most certainly do!"

Marcus dropped him. "Well, you'll answer to the Court for that." He turned, his back to the coward. "But while we're here, how about we finally settle this, once and for all." He pointed at the footprints. "Simon, if you would be so kind?"

Simon stepped forward and put his rather large feet in the far smaller footprints. He turned and smiled slightly at Gilles, still cowering against the far wall. "It's as if a baby stood here."

Roars of laughter raced through the crowd, the fear of their oppressor gone. Simon stepped back, turning to face Gilles.

Marcus looked about at the faces, pleased to see eagerness rather than fear for once. "Well, I think we've proven that Simon wasn't the one who stood

246

here, with a cane, watching as Roland bled to death." He turned to Simon. "Did you find what you were looking for?"

Simon's face turned grim and his features sagged. "We did."

Marcus held out a hand toward the door. "Lead the way."

Simon stepped toward the door and a path cleared. Gilles sank deeper into a corner but Marcus grabbed him by the arm and hauled him outside. The crowd parted for them, even Gilles' men not sure of what to do, too many smiles surrounding them, as if everyone gathered knew their suffering was about to be over.

Though any joy Marcus might have felt now was shoved aside the moment he saw the cart with David and Jeremy standing at the rear of it, a blanket covering its contents. Simon stood at the cart and made the sign of the cross as Marcus joined him, then they both turned to face the crowd now surrounding them.

"What is the story you all remember? That Simon pushed a young Christian into the river, and that he was swept away, never to be found?" The crowd nodded, almost in unison. "If that were true, then how would you explain this?" He held out his hand toward the back of the cart and motioned at Jeremy. The young squire, his face grim, removed the blanket, revealing a small skeleton with threadbare clothes still clinging to the tiny frame.

Gasps and cries echoed across the property as sobs broke out among many who had known the boy, many who probably grew up with him.

For they immediately knew whom he was.

But it still had to be said.

Marcus, his chest tight, patted Simon on the shoulder. "My good people, it is with a heavy heart that I give you the body of Christian Samuel, dead these thirty years."

"Is that my boy!" cried someone from the back, and a hushed silence swept over the crowd as it parted, an elderly woman creeping forward, supported by what might be her daughter. As the woman neared, she gasped and collapsed, her companion catching her. The woman quickly recovered and continued her approach.

She reached out a hand to touch the remains, but stopped, instead turning and burying her head in her escort's shoulder.

"Is it him, Mama?"

The old woman nodded. "It is. I recognize the clothes."

Marcus stepped forward. "I'm sorry for your loss, Mrs. Samuel."

Mrs. Samuel drew a deep breath as she tried to regain her composure. She turned to face them. "Where? Where did you find him after all this time?"

Simon stepped forward, his head hung low. "It was Gilles that pushed him that day. Into the old Tremblay well."

More gasps, and the old woman, along with the crowd, turned to Gilles, still held captive by Marcus' iron grip.

"Is this true?" asked Mrs. Samuel.

Gilles glared at Simon defiantly. "No, it's not. I mean, yes, he fell in the well, but Simon pushed him, not me."

"But why would you lie?"

Gilles scrambled for an answer. "Well, because I didn't want you to go through the pain of seeing him dead like that. I thought it was better you never find his body, so you wouldn't have to remember him like that." He glared at Simon. "Now look what you've done? Her last memory of her beloved Christian will be this, this monstrosity!"

Marcus was impressed at how quickly Gilles could think on his feet. But he was having none of it. He shoved Gilles toward David and Jeremy, who each grabbed an arm, then stepped over to the cart to examine the remains.

And suppressed a smile before returning his attention to the crowd. "Can anyone tell me what Mrs. Laurent was concerned with that night?"

He was met with confused stares.

"Perhaps more concerned about it rather than the fact a young boy had died?"

"That bloody shirt!" shouted Mathilde from the porch. "She wouldn't shut up about it!"

Marcus smiled. "Exactly. Those who were there remember it, don't you?"

There were nods among the elders.

"And what was so special about this shirt?"

"It was from Paris," said somebody.

"Made of fine Italian silk, it was!"

"A foolish extravagance bought by a foolish woman!"

Gilles bristled. "Hey, I won't have anyone speaking ill of my mother!"

Marcus held up a hand, silencing the crowd. "Of

course not, no one wants to speak ill of the dead." He returned to the matter at hand. "And why was she upset?"

"The sleeve had been ripped off," shouted someone.

Mrs. Samuel wagged a finger. "That's right!" She jabbed her bony hand at Gilles. "He said that he fought with Simon, trying to stop him from getting away after he killed my Christian." She turned to Marcus. "But what does it matter? A shirt was torn. How can you prove who killed my boy after all these years?"

Marcus smiled at her. "All in good time, madam." He turned to the crowd. "I will ask you this. If Simon tore the shirt, is it at all likely that he would have carried the torn sleeve on his person for thirty years?"

"Ridiculous!"

"Of course not!"

Marcus held up a hand, silencing them. "And you'd be correct, of course. It is completely ridiculous to suggest that he did such a thing. Which means that, other than my sergeant planting that sleeve on the body of poor Christian today, how would you explain why a shirt sleeve, made of silk, is still gripped in Christian's hand after all these years?"

Gasps were met with a rush of people as they surged toward the cart to see the evidence for themselves. Marcus stepped aside, allowing them to see the soiled, nearly threadbare shirtsleeve, the last thing Christian had grabbed before falling into the well so long ago.

Marcus let the crowd each get a look before resuming. "So I ask you, those who were there the night Gilles told you that Simon had killed Christian by pushing him into the river, that saw Gilles' torn shirt, is this the missing piece?"

Dozens in the crowd proclaimed a resounding yes, even Mrs. Samuel agreeing.

"Then if it is in young Christian's hand, lying at the bottom of a well, who do you think pushed him? Simon, or Gilles, whose sleeve was torn from his shirt as Christian fell backward, into the well?"

Mrs. Samuel advanced on Gilles. "You killed my boy! All these years you lied! All these years I thought you were the hero, and that poor Simon here was the murderer. All these years my poor boy has lain at the bottom of a well, unable to find peace." She jabbed a finger into his chest. "You have to pay!"

"Somebody get a rope!"

Gilles struggled to free himself from David and Jeremy, then swung his head about, searching for his men. "Help me, you fools!"

But their loyalty proved fleeting, and they instead mounted their horses and fled, leaving their master to the horde they had suppressed only this morning.

"Let him go," said Marcus, and his squires released their grip. Marcus stepped back, along with the others, as the crowd descended upon Gilles, the source of all that ailed them soon lost in the melee.

Jeremy voiced the question they all silently were asking. "Should we stop this?"

Simon shook his head. "Stop what? Justice? I could forgive him for what he did to Christian, and even what he did to me for lying about it. Those were the acts of a child. But he murdered Roland in cold blood, simply to cover up a childhood accident. What happened all those years ago wasn't murder. But what he did to cover it up was. And from what Marcus has been telling me, he's acted like a tyrant to these people, abusing his power and stealing from them. How many has he killed and beaten over the years?" Simon pursed his lips as they watched a rope get tied to Gilles' own horse. "His pain will be fleeting. Unlike the scores he condemned to death through torture."

Marcus regarded his sergeant for a moment, trying to imagine what he had gone through all those weeks. He had only seen the aftermath, had never seen what they had actually done to him, and wondered if the poor man would ever truly recover.

The crowd cheered and Marcus turned to see Gilles hoisted by the neck as the horse surged forward with a smack to its hindquarters. His feet twitched, and his eyes bulged, then there was nothing.

Silence ruled the crowd as the reality of what they had done set in. They had killed a man. And they would have to live with that. Though Marcus didn't fault them for their actions, some that had gathered today would have many sleepless nights over the coming days, and he only prayed that the Lord forgave them for this sin, on their day of judgment.

"Simon!"

They all turned to see Mr. and Mrs. Chastain rush up, their faces all smiles. Mrs. Chastain hugged her son, hard, as her husband nearly crushed his hat between his hands.

"I'm so sorry we ever doubted you, son."

Simon smiled at his parents. "It's not your fault. Everyone believed him, and I ran away like a coward, rather than defend myself."

His father shook his head, reaching out tentatively to touch his son's arm. "From what I've been told, you are anything but a coward. And for your master to come looking for you, and for him to risk his life to clear your good name, you must be an honorable man." The man's lip trembled and tears filled his eyes. "You-you are a man I'm proud to call my son."

Simon's eyes glistened, and he embraced his father and mother together, Marcus and the others taking a few steps back to give them some privacy, though none was to be had that day on the Villeneuve property, as scores of people watched with smiles on their faces as a reunion, thirty years overdue, was finally properly taking place—in the shining face of truth.

Simon stepped back, a hand on each of them. "If it would be fine with you, I'd like to visit from time to time."

His father smiled. "Your mother and I would like that."

"Now I must go. I have duties to tend to."

His father beamed, then turned to face the crowd filled with neighbors that had resented the Chastain family for decades, and had shunned them, condemning them for the lies told about their son. He put an arm around Simon, tears streaking his face, his chest swelled with pride as Marcus had never seen it. "This is my son, the Templar! This is my son, Simon!"

The crowd erupted in cheers, and Marcus' chest ached at the love shown for his sergeant and his family, as the crowd rushed them, handshakes, hugs, and pats on the back exchanged with the boy they would have hanged so many years ago, had he had the

253

courage to defend himself as a child.

Marcus wasn't sure how long they waited there, but there was no way he would cut this short and deny Simon his moment of glory. He was innocent of both crimes, and it had been proven in front of all those who had condemned him, even his parents, and Christian's only surviving parent.

It felt good.

They all felt good, David and Jeremy nothing but smiles.

Simon finally extricated himself, rejoining his friends. "Get me out of here before I weep like a woman."

Marcus laughed and they all mounted their horses, waving at what remained of the dissipating crowd, and taking one final look at Gilles Laurent as he swung from the largest tree of the home of his last victim.

I wonder how long they'll leave him there.

It didn't matter. None of it was his concern anymore. He had found Simon, cleared his name, and now they were all heading home, but not before traveling one last time through Le Chesnay, the streets lined on either side with newly liberated people, smiles and laughter filling the air as they clapped at their saviors, shouting their thanks.

"I feel like I'm on parade in the Holy Land."

Marcus chuckled at Simon's observation. "It does remind one of that, doesn't it?" He regarded his sergeant. "Have you made a decision?"

Simon looked at him. "About what?"

"About living on the farm."

Simon nodded. "After what I just went through,

I'm not sure I'll ever leave it again." He stared at the road ahead, a smile on his face, and Marcus couldn't recall ever seeing the man so at peace, as if all the demons he had been wrestling with his entire life, were gone.

Approaching the de Rancourt Residence
Crécy-la-Chapelle, Kingdom of France

Marcus smiled and waved as he and Simon slowly rode through the town they now called home. There had been resistance at first to their arrival, but over the past several months, these people had come to embrace them and the good work they were doing. He was certain part of it was whom they represented, everyone probably feeling a little safer having Templars nearby to help should there be trouble, though he knew it was more than that.

He glanced at Simon, riding at his side, and his heart swelled at the broad smile on his sergeant's face, returning the waves, and for the first time that he could remember, smiling broadly at the children running alongside them.

He was a new man.

It ate him up inside knowing that his best friend had been so tortured for decades, and had kept it to himself, though perhaps that wasn't fair. It wasn't until they settled on the farm, constantly surrounded by children, that his melancholy truly set in, and his entire demeanor had changed.

But that was over now.

Simon was back.

Now the long road to recovery from what he had endured over the past month in La Conciergerie Prison would begin. And it was an ordeal from which Marcus feared his friend might never fully recover. He had seen men who had suffered at the hands of the

Saracens, and they were never the same.

He held out hope, though, as it had been only a month, and many of those men had been imprisoned for months or years before being rescued or exchanged. He only prayed that he had rescued Simon early enough. Clearing his name of both murders, and reconciling with his parents, seemed to have buoyed his spirits, and hopefully that would sustain him through the long winter ahead.

Simon's smile broadened and Marcus was pleased to see it was the first glimpse of the farm responsible. They urged their horses on a little faster, and were soon on the path leading to their humble home. Jeremy shouted from the now installed door of the barracks, waving at them, Marcus having sent his squires on ahead, since traveling with the weakened Simon would take longer.

Before they dismounted, they were surrounded by the children, their squires, the women in their lives, and their faithful companion Tanya, all tremendously relieved to see Simon.

"Thank the good Lord you're safe!" cried Lady Joanne as she gave Simon a hug, the crusty old sergeant returning it awkwardly, though with a smile. He held out a hand for Thomas Durant, standing nearby.

"I thank the good Lord for you, Master Durant. If it weren't for you, I'd likely be dead now."

Thomas flushed, but Isabelle Leblanc beamed, the young woman unable to tear her eyes away from the man, even with Marcus so close at hand.

And Marcus breathed a sigh of relief at the sight. Could it be that she had finally moved on with her infatuation of him, and found someone more appropriate to direct her attentions toward?

He would ask Lady Joanne about the goings on these past days when he had the chance.

Joanne clapped. "All right, children, let these men be. Dinner is almost ready, so clean up." The children disappeared inside the house, Tanya following. Joanne gave Marcus a hug. "It's good to have you back. All of you." She waved a hand in front of her nose. "Now you two go clean up. You need it!"

Marcus laughed, as did Simon. "Rest assured, Milady, we will be properly bathed before we see you again."

She patted him on the cheek. "Good. And eat with us in the house tonight. All of you. It will be tight quarters, but worth it just the same."

Marcus bowed. "We accept your gracious invitation."

Joanne laughed, batting him on the arm. "It's *your* house!" She shook her head as she turned away. "Oh, how I've missed you all." She put her arm around Beatrice and they disappeared inside. Marcus motioned toward Thomas.

"Walk with me."

"Y-yes, sir."

Isabelle frowned, then stood staring after them as they mounted the hill toward the barracks, as if unsure of whether she should follow. She finally chose wisely, disappearing inside the house.

"I want to thank you once again for helping save my sergeant."

Thomas stared at his feet. "It was the least I could do after all you have done for me."

"You know my invitation for you to stay with us still stands. We would be honored to have you consider this your home."

Thomas' ears went red, and he stole a quick glance at the farmhouse behind him. "I-I can't abandon my home. It's all I have left of my family." He shrugged. "Besides, things aren't so bad now that I'm making money."

Marcus regarded the young man, and even without his keen eye, he knew Thomas was troubled. "You don't seem happy."

Thomas frowned. "I still haven't come to terms with what I now do for a living."

"Does Mrs. Thibault have you do things you aren't comfortable with?"

He shook his head. "Not really. I mean, I never have to do anything bad. All I do is read letters, write responses, and tally her books. But I hear the treachery through the walls of my office as the people file through every day, either falling into her clutches, or desperately trying to escape. And it's my numbers…"

His voice drifted off and Marcus could tell the young man was about to lose control. "Perhaps if it troubles you so, you shouldn't do it."

Thomas sighed. "I keep thinking that maybe there's something I can do to help these people. Maybe I could tally the numbers incorrectly in their favor, grant them a small reprieve."

Marcus shook his head. "I wouldn't do that. If Mrs. Thibault found out, it could be your head."

Thomas nodded. "I know, which is why I haven't had the courage to do anything. Instead, I focus on making sure the numbers are accurate, and never erroneously in Mrs. Thibault's favor."

Simon looked at Thomas. "You need to ask yourself if your mother and father would be proud of what you're doing."

Thomas flushed, his eyes glistening. "I know my mother would be ashamed, I'm sure. And my father?" His shoulders slumped. "My father was never an honest man, though never a bad man. But isn't what he did the same as what I'm doing now? He created the documents, as I tally the numbers. Innocent people got hurt by those forgeries, but never by his hand. Would he be proud? I doubt it. But could he fault me for what I've been forced to do? Not without being a hypocrite."

Simon patted Thomas on the shoulder. "I think you have your answer, don't you?"

Thomas stared at him for a moment then stopped. "I know what the right thing to do is. I know coming here is what I should be doing." He stared down at the house. "And Isabelle…"

Marcus and Simon exchanged a quick glance, Marcus suppressing a smile as his read on the situation was proven correct. He placed a hand on Thomas' shoulder. "You have plenty of time to decide." He looked at Simon. "We're not going anywhere, are we?"

Simon smiled broadly, drawing a long breath as he surveyed the area. "Not if I have anything to say about it."

Marcus' chest ached with the relief he felt over those words, and the fact he finally believed them with respect to the decision foisted upon them all. They were all staying, and they were all staying willingly, and for that, he was grateful, though the price to come to that decision had been high.

Thomas stared at them for a moment. "If there is one good thing that came out of me working for Mrs. Thibault, it is that I was able to hear of your suffering. Perhaps I can use my position for some good, and be of service to you in the future."

Marcus regarded him. "Are you sure?"

Thomas laughed, a laugh tainted with uncertainty. "No, but it's a reasonable excuse to not make a decision now, isn't it? What lies back in Paris is my home. It's all I've ever known, and all I have left of my family, and I'm not ready yet to let that go."

Marcus squeezed the man's shoulder. "You are a good man, Thomas Durant. Never forget that, no matter how you feel about the work you've been forced to do. In time, you will decide the right path for you, and should it bring you here, we will embrace you as a brother."

Thomas' eyes glistened. "Perhaps one day, assuming I don't lose my soul to Mrs. Thibault."

Marcus frowned. "Do you think that's a possibility?"

Thomas stared at his feet. "The money is better than I could have ever imagined, so much so that I'm already repairing the house, but one day, I fear she'll ask of me something I would refuse today, but tomorrow I'll have become so accustomed to the money, that I'll cross a line I never thought possible." He stared up at the heavens. "I can only pray that when that day comes, I recognize it, and come here, instead of crossing over to a darkness I fear there may be no returning from."

261

Marcus nodded, a frown creasing his face. "You have much to think about, Master Durant. And should you ever need a place to escape to, even if for only a day, you are always welcome here."

"Thomas, dinner!"

They all turned to see Isabelle waving from the doorway, and Marcus caught the huge smile on Thomas' face. He patted the young man on the back. "You better go to her."

"Yes, sir." Thomas sprinted down the hill, almost losing his footing a couple of times, but reached the doorway safely, the smiles of two young lovers evident even from here.

Simon grunted. "I fear for his soul."

"As do I. But what can we do?"

Simon turned back toward their barracks, and they both continued up the hill. "Burn down his house?"

Marcus chuckled. "This morning, I would have said it might have to come to that. But I think it will be his burning heart that will bring him back to us, not a burning home."

Simon slapped him on the back. "I bet you're thanking the good Lord right now that you're off Isabelle's mind!"

Marcus laughed. "You have no idea! It's proof indeed that He hears our prayers!"

THE END

ACKNOWLEDGMENTS

It took me finishing this novel before I remembered a painful event from my childhood. It took place when I was six or seven years old. We were stationed in Goose Bay, Labrador, where eleven months of the year there was good snowmobiling, and one month of summer. Good times if you're a kid who loves snow.

But something tragic happened one day, and it wasn't until I went out for a drive this very morning, that I remembered it, and decided to update these acknowledgments.

I have three distinct memories of this event. The first is my friends asking me to go with them, and me saying no. The second is the mother of one of those friends ringing our doorbell later that day, looking for her son. And the third is his funeral, several days later.

It was my first experience with death, and I have absolutely no memories of how I felt about it at the time. I assume I was sad. After all, this was one of my best friends.

But I can't even remember his name.

So why did this book bring those memories back?

My friend died, not because he fell through the ice on a river, but because my other friend did. My friend dove in after him, pulled him to safety, but died from the efforts, probably from hypothermia. I just finished speaking to my father about it, and he said the doctor tried for hours to save him, but it was no use.

He was gone.

He died a hero, saving the other boy, saving his friend, and now, forty years later, I can't even remember his name, and that crushes me, probably more than a young six-year-old could have fathomed back then.

To my friend, I say this: I'm sorry I forgot you, but now I'll never forget.

And now for something a *lot* lighter.

People drink.

They always have, and they always will. And once they figured out that water wasn't the only thing they could quench their thirst with, concoctions were created over the millennia, including various alcohols, hot and cold beverages, and my personal favorite.

Diet Doctor Pepper.

Oh yeah! Love that stuff!

But what did thirteenth-century people enjoy? Coffee hadn't yet been discovered by Europeans, nor had tea.

Enter the tisane.

Until I started writing this series, I had no idea what a tisane was, beyond knowing that Hercule Poirot loved it, and would always order it on the television series, or in the pages of the original novels by the great Agatha Christie.

Yet it was always just a word until I looked up what people drank in thirteenth-century France. Among other things, tisanes were popular.

So what the heck is a tisane?

It's an "infusion," made in a way quite similar to tea, but with herbs and spices left to soak in boiling hot water, rather than tea leaves. I have no idea if it is any good, nor shall I probably ever find out. I can't stand hot drinks. I've never had beyond a sip of coffee or tea in my entire life, and I don't even like hot chocolate, though apparently I did as a child.

It's ice cold for me, which means I probably would have hated the Dark Ages—for lots of reasons I'm sure beyond the lack of ice cubes.

As usual, there are people to thank. My dad, as always, for the research, and Deborah Wilson for some equine info. And, of course, my wife, daughter, mother, and friends, for their continued support, and a special thanks to the proofreading and launch teams!

To those who have not already done so, please visit my website at www.jrobertkennedy.com, then sign up for the Insider's Club to be notified of new book releases. Your email address will never be shared or sold.

Thank you once again for reading.

Printed in the USA
CPSIA information can be obtained
at www.ICGtesting.com
LVHW030746160124
769002LV00019B/1473

9 781990 418020